A PEEP BEHIND THE SCENES

A PEEP BEHIND THE SCENES

By

MRS. O. F. WALTON

Author of
' *Christies Old Organ* ' *etc.*

Republished by:
A. B. Publishing, Inc.
Ithaca, Mi 48847
Cover Art:
James Converse
copyright 1997
by A. B. Publishing

A NOTE TO THE PUBLIC

In November, 1894, D. L. Moody founded what was known as "The Bible Institute Colportage Association". The purpose of the association was as follows, and I quote:

1. To produce good literature at a price within the reach of all.

2. To carry the Gospel by means of the printed page, where church privileges are wanting or not embraced.

3. To supply suitable religious reading for distribution among all classes, young and old.

4. To provide a profitable means of employment.

Liberal terms are made to colporters and canvassers. Previous experience not essential. Full printed instructions and suggestions provided. All of one's time need not be given, but the more the better.

Ten Reasons for Engaging in the Colportage Work

1. It is God's work, pre-eminently so, in its aim, method and blessing attendant. It is a definite form of *Christian work*, not merely book-selling.

2. It carries the Gospel into thousands of homes where pastors or other Christian workers do not usually, or cannot go.

3. By it the greatest amount of good, though direct contact, can be done to the largest number.

4. It presents countless opportunities for doing personal work and for enlisting men's lives and sympathies in the cause of Christ.

5. It supplements all other evangelical agencies for the promotion of the kingdom of God among men. There need be no fear of rivalry or competition; Christian colporters are wanted everywhere.

6. It may be undertaken in so great variety of ways--home to home, churches, societies, conventions, mail, lectures, etc.

7. The plan of Colportage visiting or "book missionary" work is applicable anywhere, city, town and country.

8. The work is not an experiment, but an established and thoroughly tried method of *reaching the people*, especially those who do not go to church nor care for religious things.

9. The opportunity offered to travel, see the country and meet people of all classes.

10. It provides paying employment at the smallest outlay of money, and the least possible risk of failure or loss. The remuneration offered is liberal and in proportion to the amount of time and energy expended. Diligent and consecrated men and women make all expenses and enough more to provide a reserve fund. End of quote.

CONTENTS

5

CHAPTER I

ROSALIE

RAIN, rain, rain! How mercilessly it fell on the fair-field that Sunday afternoon! Every moment the pools increased and the mud became thicker. How dismal the fair looked then! On Saturday evening it had been brilliantly lighted, and the grand shows in the most aristocratic part of the field had been illuminated with crosses, star anchors, and all manner of devices.

There were no lights now; there was nothing to cast a halo round the dirty, weather-stained tents and the dingy caravans.

Yet, in spite of this, and in spite of the rain, a crowd of Sunday idlers lingered about the fair, looking with great interest at the half-covered whirligigs and bicycles, peeping curiously into the deserted shows, and making many schemes for further enjoyment on the morrow, when the fair was once more to be in its glory.

Inside the caravans the show-people were crouching over their fires and grumbling at the weather, murmuring at having to pay so much for the ground on which their shows were erected, at a time when they would be likely to make so little profit.

A little old man, with a rosy, good-tempered face, was making his way across the sea of mud which divided the shows from each other. He was evidently no idler in the fair; he had come into it that

Sunday afternoon for a definite purpose, and he did not intend to leave it until it was accomplished. After crossing an almost impassable place he climbed the steps leading to one of the caravans and knocked at the door.

It was a curious door; the upper part of it, being used as a window, was filled with glass, behind which you could see two small muslin curtains, tied up with pink ribbon. No one came to open the door when the old man knocked, and he was about to turn away, when some little boys, who were standing near, called out to him:

'Rap again, sir, rap again; there's a little lass in there; she went in a bit since.'

'Don't you wish you was her?' said one of the little boys to the other.

'Ay!' said the little fellow, 'I wish *our* house would move about, and had little windows with white curtains and pink bows!'

The old man laughed a hearty laugh at the children's talk, and rapped again at the caravan door.

This time a face appeared between the muslin curtains and peered cautiously out. It was a very pretty little face, so pretty that the old man sighed to himself when he saw it.

Then the small head turned round, and seemed to be telling what it had seen to someone within, and asking leave to admit the visitor; for a minute afterwards the door was opened, and the owner of the pretty face stood before the old man.

She was a little girl about twelve years of age, very slender and delicate in appearance. Her hair,

which was of a rich auburn colour, was hanging
down to her waist, and her eyes were the most
beautiful the old man thought he had ever seen.

She was very poorly dressed, and she shivered
as the damp, cold air rushed in through the open
door.

'Good afternoon, my little dear,' said the old man.

She was just going to answer him when a violent
fit of coughing from within caused her to look
round, and when it was over, a weak, querulous
voice said hurriedly:

'Shut the door, Rosalie; it's so cold; ask whoever
it is to come in.'

The old man did not wait for a second invitation;
he stepped inside the caravan, and the child closed
the door.

It was a very small place. At the end of the
caravan was a narrow bed something like a berth
on board ship, and on it a woman was lying who
was evidently very ill. She was the child's mother,
the old man felt sure. She had the same beautiful
eyes and sunny hair, though her face was thin and
wasted.

There was not room for much furniture in the
small caravan; a tiny stove, the chimney of which
went through the wooden roof, a few pans, a shelf
containing cups and saucers, and two boxes which
served as seats, completely filled it. There was only,
just room for the old man to stand, and the fire
was so near him that he was in danger of being
scorched.

Rosalie had seated herself on one of the boxes
close to her mother's bed.

'You must excuse my intruding, ma'am,' said the old man, with a polite bow; 'but I'm so fond of little folks, and I've brought this little girl of yours a picture, if she will accept it from me.'

A flush of pleasure came into the child's face as he brought out of his pocket his promised gift. She seized it eagerly, and held it up before her with evident delight, while her mother raised herself on her elbow to look at it also.

It was the picture of a shepherd, with a very kind and compassionate face, who was bearing home in his bosom a lost lamb. The lamb's fleece was torn in several places, and there were marks of blood on its back as if it had been roughly used by some cruel beast in a recent struggle.

The shepherd seemed to have suffered more than the lamb, for he was wounded in many places, and his blood was falling in large drops on the ground. Yet he did not seem to mind it; his face was full of love and full of joy as he looked at the lamb. He had forgotten his sorrow in his joy that the lamb was saved.

In the distance were some of the shepherd's friends, who were coming to meet him, and underneath the picture were these words, printed in large letters:

'Rejoice with Me, for I have found My sheep which was lost. There is joy in the presence of the angels of God over one sinner that repenteth.'

The little girl read the words aloud in a clear, distinct voice; and her mother gazed at the picture with tears in her eyes.

'Those are sweet words, ain't they?' said the old man.

'Yes,' said the woman with a sigh; 'I have heard them many times before.'

'Has the Good Shepherd ever said them of *you*, ma'am? Has He ever called the bright angels together and said to them of *you*, "Rejoice with Me, for I have found My sheep which was lost"?'

The woman did not speak; a fit of coughing came on, and the old man stood looking at her with a very pitying expression.

'You are very ill, ma'am, I'm afraid,' he said.

'Yes, very ill,' gasped the woman, bitterly; 'every one can see that but Augustus!'

'That's my father,' said the little girl.

'No; he doesn't see it,' repeated the woman; 'he thinks I ought to get up and act in the play just as usual. I did try at the last place we went to; but I fainted as soon as my part was over, and I've been in bed ever since.'

'You must be tired of moving about, ma'am,' said the old man, compassionately.

'Tired!' said she; 'I should think I *was* tired; it isn't what I was brought up to. I was brought up to a very different kind of life from *this*,' she said, with a very deep-drawn sigh; 'it's a weary time I have of it—a weary time.'

'Are you always on the move, ma'am?' asked the old man.

'All the summer-time,' said the woman. 'We get into lodgings for a little time in the winter; and then we let ourselves out to some of the small town theatres; but all the rest of the year we're going from fair to fair—no rest nor comfort, not a bit!'

'Poor thing! poor thing!' said the old man; and then a choking sensation appeared to have seized him, for he cleared his throat vigorously many times, but seemed unable to say more.

The child had climbed on one of the boxes, and brought down a square red pin-cushion from the shelf which ran round the top of the caravan. From this she took two pins, and fastened the picture on the wooden wall, so that her mother could see it as she was lying in bed.

'It does look pretty there,' said the little girl; 'mummy, you can look at it nicely now!'

'Yes, ma'am,' said the old man, as he prepared to take his leave; 'and as you look at it, think of the Good Shepherd Who is seeking you. He wants to find you, and take you up in His arms, and carry you home; and He won't mind the wounds it has cost Him, if you'll only let Him do it. Good-day, ma'am,' said the old man; 'I shall, maybe, never see you again; but I would like the Good Shepherd to say those words of you.'

He went carefully down the steps of the caravan, and Rosalie stood at the window, watching him picking his way to the other shows, to which he was carrying the same message of peace. She looked out from between the muslin curtains until he had quite disappeared to a distant part of the field, and then she turned to her mother and said eagerly:

'It's a very pretty picture, isn't it, mummy dear?'

No answer came from the bed. Rosalie thought her mother was asleep, and crept on tiptoe to her side, fearful of waking her. But she found her mother's face buried in the pillow on which large tears were falling.

When the little girl sat down by her side, and tried to comfort her by stroking her hand very gently, and saying: 'Mummy dear, mummy dear, don't cry! What's the matter, mummy dear?' her mother only wept the more.

At length her sobs brought on such a violent fit of coughing that Rosalie was much alarmed, and fetched her a mug of water, which was standing on the shelf near the door. By degrees her mother grew calmer, the sobs became less frequent, and to the little girl's joy, she fell asleep. Rosalie sat beside her without moving, lest she should awake her, and kept gazing at her picture till she knew every line of it. And the first thing her mother heard when she awoke from sleep was Rosalie's voice saying softly:

'"Rejoice with Me, for I have found My sheep which was lost. There is joy in the presence of the angels of God over one sinner that repenteth".'

THE LITTLE THEATRE

IT was the next evening; the fair was once more in its glory, and crowded with an admiring throng. The great shows were again illuminated, and three rows of brilliant stars shone forth from the little theatre belonging to Rosalie's father. He had been out all day, strolling about the town, and had only returned in time to make preparation for the evening's entertainment.

'Norah!' said her husband, as he put his head in at the door of the caravan, 'surely you mean to come and take your part to-night?'

'I can't, Augustus, and you would know it, if you stayed long enough with me; I've been coughing nearly the whole day.'

'Well, I wish you would get better soon; it's very awkward to have to fill your part up every time; Conrad has to take it, and every one can see he's not used to it, he's so clumsy and slow.'

'I'll come as soon as ever I can,' said the poor wife with a sigh.

'It's to be hoped you will,' said her husband. 'Women are always fancying they are ill; they lie still thinking about it, and nursing themselves up, long after a man would have been at his work again; it's half laziness, that's what it is!' said Augustus fiercely.

'If you felt as ill as I do, Augustus,' said his wife, 'I'm sure you wouldn't do any work.'

'Hold your tongue!' said her husband; 'I know better than that. Well, mind you have Rosalie ready in time; we shall begin early to-night.'

Little Rosalie had crept to her mother's side, and was crying quietly at her father's rough words.

'Stop crying this minute, child!' said Augustus, harshly; 'wipe your eyes, you great baby! Do you think you'll be fit to come on the stage, if they're red and swollen with crying? Do you hear me? Stop at once, or it will be the worse for you,' he shouted, as he shut the caravan door.

'Rosalie, darling,' said her mother, 'you mustn't cry; your father will be so angry; and it's time you got ready. What a noise there is in the fair already!' said the poor woman, holding her aching head.

Rosalie wiped her eyes and washed her face, and then brought out from one of the boxes the dress in which she was to act at the play. It was a white muslin dress, looped up with pink roses, and there was a wreath of paper roses to wear in her hair. She dressed herself before a tiny looking-glass, and then went to her mother to have the wreath of roses fastened on her head.

The poor woman raised herself in bed, and arranged her little girl's long tresses.

What a contrast Rosalie looked to the rest of the caravan! The shabby furniture, the thin, wasted mother, the dirty, torn little frock she had just laid aside, were quite out of keeping with the pretty little white-robed figure which stood by the bed.

At length her father's voice called her, and after giving her mother a last kiss, and after placing some water near her on the box, in case a violent fit of coughing should come on, Rosalie ran quickly down the caravan steps and rushed into the brilliantly-lighted theatre. A crowd of people stared at her as she flitted past and disappeared up the theatre steps.

The audience had not yet been admitted, so Rosalie crept into the room behind the stage in which her father's company was assembled. They all looked tired and cross, for this was the last night of the fair, and they had little sleep while it lasted.

At last Augustus announced that it was time to begin, and they all went out on the platform, which was erected half-way up the outside of the theatre, just underneath the three rows of illuminated stars. Here they danced, and sang, and shook tambourines, in order to beguile the people to enter. Then they disappeared within, and a crowd of eager spectators immediately rushed up the steps, paid their admission money, and took their seats in the theatre.

After this the play commenced, Augustus acting as manager, and keeping his company up to their various parts. It was a foolish play, and in some of the parts there was a strong mixture of objectionable language; yet it was highly appreciated by the audience, and met with vociferous applause.

There were many young girls there, some of them servants in respectable families, where they enjoyed every comfort; yet they looked up at little Rosalie with eyes of admiration and envy. They thought her life was much happier than theirs, and that her lot was greatly to be desired. They looked at the white dress and the pink roses, and contrasted them with their own warm but homely garments; they watched the pretty girl going through her part gracefully and easily, and they contrasted her work with theirs. How interesting, how delightful, they thought, to be doing this, instead of scrubbing floors, or washing clothes, or nursing children!

They knew nothing of the life behind the scenes, of the sick mother, the wretched home, the poor and insufficient food, the dirty, ragged frock. They knew nothing of the bitter tears which had just been wiped away, nor of the weary aching of the little feet which were dancing so lightly over the stage.

The little feet became more and more weary as the night went on. As soon as the play was over the people rushed out into the fair to seek for fresh amusement. But the actors had no rest. Once more they appeared on the platform, to attract a fresh audience, and then the same play was repeated, the same songs were sung, the same words were said; fresh to the people who were listening, but oh! how stale and monotonous to the actors themselves!

So it went on; as soon as one exhibition was over another began, and the theatre was filled and refilled, long after the clock of the neighbouring church had struck the hour of twelve.

At last it was over; the last audience had left, the brilliant stars disappeared, and Rosalie was at liberty to creep back to her mother. So weary and exhausted was she, that she could hardly drag herself up the caravan steps. She opened the door very gently, that she might not disturb her mother, and then she tried to undress herself. But she was aching in every limb, and, sitting down on the

B

box beside her mother's bed, she fell asleep, her little weary head resting on her mother's pillow.

Poor little woman! She ought to have been laid in a quiet little nest hours ago, instead of being exposed to the hot, stifling air of the theatre through all the long hours of a weary night.

In about an hour's time her mother woke, and found her little girl sleeping in her uncomfortable position, her white dress unfastened, and the pink roses from her hair fallen on the ground. Weak as she was, the poor mother dragged herself out of bed to help her tired child to undress.

'Rosalie, dear,' she said, tenderly, 'wake up.'

For some time Rosalie did not stir, and, when her mother touched her, she sat up, and said, as if in her sleep:

'"Rejoice with Me, for I have found My sheep which was lost."'

'She is dreaming of her picture, poor child!' said the mother to herself.

Then Rosalie woke, and shivered as she felt the cold night air on her bare neck and arms. Very gently the poor weak mother helped her to take off her white dress and her small ragged petticoats; and then the child crept into bed and into her mother's arms.

'Poor little tired lamb!' said the mother as the weary child nestled up to her.

'Am I the lamb?' said Rosalie, in a sleepy voice.

The mother did not answer, but kissed her child passionately, and then lay awake by her side, weeping and coughing by turns till the morning dawned.

CHAPTER 3

THE DAY AFTER THE FAIR

THE next morning Rosalie was waked by a rap at the caravan door. She crept out of bed and, putting her dress over her shoulders, peeped out between the muslin curtains.

'It's Toby, mummy,' she said; 'I'll see what he wants.'

She opened the door a crack, and Toby put his mouth to it, and whispered: 'Miss Rosie, we're going to start in about half an hour. Master has just sent me for the horses; we've been up all night packing; three of the wagons is loaded, and they've only some of the scenery to roll up, and then we shall start.'

'Where are we going, Toby?' asked the child.

'It's a town a long way off,' said Toby; 'we've never been there before, master says, and it will take us nearly a week to get there. But I must be off, Miss Rosie, or master will be coming.'

'Aren't you tired, Toby?' said the child kindly.

Toby shrugged his shoulders, and said, with a broad grin:

'I wonder if any one in this concern is ever anything else but tired!'

Then he walked away into the town for the horses, which had been put up in the stables of an inn, and Rosalie returned to her mother. There were several things to be done before they could start; the crockery had all to be taken from the shelf and stowed away in a safe place, lest the jolting over the rough and uneven field should throw it down. Besides this, Rosalie had to dress herself and get her mother's breakfast ready, that she might eat it in peace before the shaking of the caravan commenced.

When all was ready, Rosalie stood at the window and looked out. The fair looked very different from what it had done the night before. Most of the show-people had been up all night, taking their shows to pieces, and packing everything up. Though it was not yet nine o'clock, many of them had already started, and the field was half empty. It was a dreary scene of desolation. The little grass it had once possessed, which had given it a right to the name of field, had entirely disappeared. Very dirty and untidy and forlorn it looked, as Rosalie gazed at it from the door of the caravan.

Then a wagon jolted past, laden with the largest of the numerous whirligigs, the wooden horses and elephants peeping out from the waterproof covering which had been thrown over them. Next a large swing passed, then the show of the giant and dwarf; these were followed by a pea-boiling establishment and the marionettes. A few minutes later the show of the blue horse and the performing seal set out on its way to the next fair, accompanied by the shows of the fat boy, and of the woman without arms, who performed wonders with her toes in the way of tea-making and other household business, and whose very infirmities and deformities were thus made into gain, and exposed to the gaze of curious crowds by her own relatives.

All these rattled past, and Rosalie watched them out of sight. Then Toby returned with the horses; they were yoked to the wagons and to the caravans, and the little cavalcade set forth. The jolting over the rough ground was very great, and much tried the poor sick woman, who was shaken from side to side of her wretched bed. Then outside the field they had to wait a long time, for the road was completely filled by the numerous caravans of the wild-beast show, and no one could pass until they were gone.

The elephants were standing close to the pavement, now and again twisting their long trunks into the trees of the small gardens in front of the neighbouring houses; and they would undoubtedly have broken the branches to atoms had not their keeper driven them off with his whip. A crowd of children was gathered round them, feeding them with bread and biscuit, and enjoying the delay of the show.

Augustus became very impatient, for he had a long·journey before him; so, after pacing up and down and chafing against the stoppage for some time, he went up to the manager of the wild-beast show and addressed him in such violent and passionate language that a policeman was obliged to interfere, and desired him to keep the peace.

At length the huge yellow caravans, each drawn by six strong cart-horses, moved slowly on, led by a procession of elephants and camels, and followed by a large crowd of children who accompanied them to the outskirts of the town. Here, by turning down a by-street, the theatre party were able to pass them, and thus get the start of them on their journey.

Rosalie was glad to leave the town and feel the fresh country air blowing on her face. It was so very refreshing after the close air of the fair. She opened the upper part of the door and stood looking out, watching Toby, who was driving, and talking to him from time to time of the objects which they passed by the way; it was a new road to Rosalie and to her mother.

About twelve o'clock, they came to a little village where they halted for a short time that the horses might rest before going farther. The country children were just leaving the village school, and they gathered round the caravans with open eyes and mouths, staring curiously at the smoke coming from the small chimneys, and at Rosalie, who was peeping out from between the muslin curtains. But, after satisfying their curiosity, they moved away in little groups to their various homes, that they might be in time to get their dinner done before afternoon school.

Then the village street was quite quiet, and Rosalie stood at the door watching the birds hopping from tree to tree, and the bees gathering honey from the flowers in the gardens. Her mother was better to-day, and was dressing herself slowly, for she thought that a breath of country air might revive and strengthen her.

Augustus, Toby, and the other men of the company had gone into the small inn for refreshment, and Toby was sent back to the caravan with large slices of bread and cheese for Rosalie and her mother. The child ate of it eagerly—the fresh air had given her an appetite—but the poor woman could not touch it. As soon as she was dressed she crept, with Rosalie's help, to the door of the caravan, and sat on the top step, leaning against one of the boxes, which the child dragged from its place to make a support for her.

The caravan was drawn up by the side of a small cottage with a thatched roof. There was a little garden in front of it, filled with sweet flowers, large cabbage-roses, southernwood, rosemary, sweet-briar, and lavender. As the wind blew softly over them, it wafted their sweet fragrance to the sick woman sitting on the caravan steps. The quiet stillness of the country was very refreshing and soothing, after the turmoil and din of the last week. No sound was to be heard but the singing of the larks overhead, the humming of the bees, and the gentle rustling of the breeze among the branches.

Then the cottage door opened, and a little child, about three years old, ran out with a ball in his hand, which he rolled down the path leading to the garden gate. A minute afterwards a young woman, in a clean cotton gown and white apron, brought her work outside, and, sitting on the seat near the cottage door, watched her child at play. She was knitting a little red sock for one of those tiny feet to wear. Click! click! click! went her knitting-needles; but she kept her eyes on the child, ready to run to him at the first alarm, to pick him up if he should fall, or to soothe him if he should be in trouble.. Now and then she glanced at the caravan standing at her garden gate, and gave a look of compassion at the poor, thin woman, whose cough from time to time was so distressing. Then, as was her custom, she began to sing as she worked; she had a clear, sweet voice, and the sick woman and her child listened.

The words of her song were these:

> 'Jesus, I Thy face am seeking,
>   Early will I turn to Thee:
> Words of love Thy voice is speaking,
>   "Come, come to Me.
>
> "Come to Me when life is dawning,
>   I thy dearest friend would be;
> In the sunshine of the morning,
>   Come, come to Me.
>
> "Come to Me—oh! do believe Me,
>   I have shed My blood for thee;
> I am waiting to receive thee,
>   Come, come to Me."
>
> Lord, I come without delaying,
>   To thine arms at once I flee,
> Lest no more I hear Thee saying,
>   "Come, come to Me."'

When she had finished singing, all was quite still again; there was hardly a sound except the pattering of the little feet on the garden path. But presently the child began to cry, and the careful mother flew to his side to discover what had pained him. It was only the loss of his ball, which he had thrown too high, and which had gone over the

hedge, and seemed to him lost for ever. Only his
ball! And yet that ball was as much to that tiny
mind as our most precious treasures are to us.

The mother knew this, so she calmed the child's
fears, and ran immediately to recover his lost play-
thing.

But Rosalie was before her. She had seen the
ball come over the hedge, and had heard the child's
cry; and when his mother appeared at the gate,
she saw the child of the caravan returning from
her chase after the ball, which had rolled some
way down the hilly road. She brought it to the
young mother, who thanked her for her kindness,
and then gazed lovingly and pityingly into her
face. She was a mother, and she thought of the
happy life her child led, compared with that of
this poor little wanderer. With this feeling in her
heart, after restoring the ball to the once more
contented child, she ran into the house, and returned
with a mug of new milk, and a slice of bread,
spread with fresh country butter, which she handed
to Rosalie and begged her to eat.

'Thank you, ma'am,' said little Rosalie; 'but
please may mummy have it? I've had some bread
and cheese; but she is too ill to eat that, and this
would do her such good.'

'Yes, to be sure,' said the kind-hearted country-
woman; 'give her that, child, and I'll fetch some
more for you.'

So it came to pass that Rosalie and her mother
had quite a little picnic on the steps of the caravan;
with the young woman standing by, and talking
to them as they ate, and now and then looking

over the hedge into the garden, that she might see if any trouble had come to her boy.

'I liked to hear you sing!' said Rosalie's mother.

'Did you?' said the young woman. 'I often sing when I'm knitting; my little one likes to hear me, and he almost knows that hymn now. Often when he is at play I hear him singing, "Tome, tome to me," so prettily, the little dear!' she said, with tears in her eyes.

'I wish *I* knew it,' said Rosalie.

'I'll tell you what,' said the young woman, 'I'll give you a card with it on; our clergyman had it printed, and we've got two of them.'

She ran again into the house, and returned with a card, on which the hymn was printed in clear, distinct type. There were two holes pierced through the top of the card, and a piece of blue ribbon had been slipped through, and tied in a bow at the top. Rosalie seized it eagerly, and began reading it at once.

'We've got such a good clergyman here,' said the young woman; 'he has not been here more than a few months, and he has done so many nice things for us. Mrs. Leslie reads aloud in one of the cottages once a week; and we all take our work and go to listen to her, and she talks to us out of the Bible; it always does me good to go.'

She stopped suddenly, as she saw Rosalie's mother's face. She had turned deadly pale, and was leaning back against the box with her eyes fixed on her.

'What's the matter, ma'am?' said the kind-hearted little woman. 'I'm afraid you've turned faint; and how you do tremble! Let me help you in; you'd better lie on your bed, hadn't you?'

She gave her her arm, and she and Rosalie took her inside the caravan, and laid her on her bed. But she was obliged to leave her in a minute or two, as her little boy was climbing on the gate, and she was afraid he would fall.

A few minutes afterwards a great noise was heard in the distance, and a number of the village children appeared, running in front of the wild-beast show, which was just passing through. The young woman took her little boy in her arms, and held him up, that he might see the elephants and camels, which were marching with stately dignity in front of the yellow vans.

When they had gone, Toby appeared with the horse, and said his master had told him he was to start, and he would follow presently with the rest of the wagons. The horse was soon put in the caravan, and they were just starting, when the young woman gathered a nosegay of the lovely flowers in her garden, and handed them to Rosalie, saying, 'Take them, and put them in water for your mother; the sight of them maybe will do her good. You'll learn the hymn, won't you? Good-bye, and God bless you!'

She watched them out of sight, standing at her cottage door with her child in her arms, whilst Rosalie leaned out of the window to nod to her and smile at her.

Then they turned a corner and came into the main street of the village.

'Can you see the church, Rosalie?' asked her mother hurriedly.

'Yes, mummy dear,' said Rosalie; 'it's just at the end of this street. Such a pretty church, with trees all round it!'

'Are there any houses near it?' asked her mother.

'Only one, mummy dear, a big house in a garden; but I can't see it very well, there are so many trees in front of it.'

'Ask Toby to put you down, Rosalie, and run and have a look at it as we pass.'

Toby lifted Rosalie down from the caravan, and she ran up to the vicarage gate, while her mother raised herself on her elbow to see as much as she could through the open window. But she could only see the spire of the church, and the chimneys of the house, and she was too exhausted to get up.

Presently Rosalie overtook them, panting with her running. Toby never dared to wait for her, lest his master should find fault with him for stopping; but Rosalie often got down from the caravan to gather wild flowers, or to drink at a wayside spring, and, as she was very fleet of foot, she was always able to overtake them.

'What was it like, Rosalie?' asked her mother, when she was seated on the box beside her bed.

'Oh! ever so pretty, mummy dear; such soft grass and such lovely roses, and a broad gravel walk all up to the door. And in the garden there was a woman; such a pretty, kind-looking woman; and she and her little girl were gathering some of the flowers.'

'Did they see you, Rosalie?'

'Yes; the little girl saw me, mummy, peeping through the gate, and she said, "Who is that little girl, mummy? I never saw her before." And then her mummy looked up and smiled at me; and she was just coming to speak to me when I turned frightened, and I saw the caravan had gone out of sight; so I ran away, and I have been running ever since to get up to you.'

The mother listened to her child's account with a pale and restless face. Then she lay back on her pillow and sighed several times.

At last they heard a rumbling sound behind them, and Toby announced, 'It's master; he's soon overtaken us.'

'Rosalie,' said her mother anxiously, 'don't you ever tell your father about that house, or that I told you to go and look at it, or about what that young woman said. Mind you never say a word to him about it; promise me, Rosalie.'

'Why not, mummy dear?' asked Rosalie, with a very perplexed face.

'Never mind why, Rosalie,' said her mother, fretfully; 'I don't wish it.'

'Very well, mummy dear,' said Rosalie.

'I'll tell you some time, Rosalie,' said her mother, gently, a minute or two afterwards; 'not to-day, though; I can't tell it to-day.'

Rosalie wondered very much what her mother meant, and she sat watching her pale, sorrowful face as she lay on her bed with her eyes closed. What was she thinking of? What was it she had to tell her? For some time Rosalie sat quite still, musing on what her mother had said, and then she pinned the card on the wall just over her dear picture, and once more read the words of the hymn.

After this she arranged the flowers in a small glass, and put them on the box near her mother's bed. The sweet-briar and cabbage-roses and southernwood filled the caravan with their fragrance. Then Rosalie took up her usual position at the door to watch Toby driving, and to see all that was to be seen by the way.

They passed through several other villages, and saw many lone farm-houses and solitary cottages. When night came they drew up on the outskirts of a small market-town. Toby took the horses to an inn, and they rested there for the night.

CHAPTER 4

THE ACTRESS'S STORY

THE next morning, as soon as it was light, the horses were put in again, and the theatre party proceeded on their way. Rosalie's mother seemed much better; the country air and country quiet had for a time restored to her much of her former strength. She was able, with Rosalie's help, to dress herself, and to sit on one of the boxes beside her bed, resting her head against the pillows, and gazing out at the green fields and clear blue sky. The sweet fresh breezes came in at the open door, and fanned her careworn face and the face of the child who sat beside her.

'Rosalie,' said her mother suddenly, 'would you like to hear about the time when your mother was a little girl?'

'Yes, mummy dear,' said Rosalie, nestling up to her side; 'I know nothing at all about it.'

'No, Rosalie,' said her mother; 'it's the beginning of a very sad story, and I did not like my little girl to know about it; but I sometimes think I shan't be long with you; and I had rather tell it to you myself than have any one else tell it. And you're getting a great girl now, Rosalie; you will be able to understand many things you could not have understood before. And there have been things the last few days which have brought it all back to me, and made me think of it by day and dream of it by night.'

'Please tell me, mummy dear,' said Rosalie, as her mother stopped speaking.

'Would you like to hear it now?' said the poor woman, with a sigh, as if she hardly liked to begin.

'Please, mummy dear,' said Rosalie.

'Then draw closer to me, child, for I don't want Toby to hear; and, mind, you must never speak of what I'm going to tell you before your father; *never*—promise me, Rosalie,' she said, earnestly.

'No, never, mummy dear,' said little Rosalie.

There was silence for a minute or two—no sound to be heard but the cracking of Toby's whip and the rumbling of the wagons behind.

'Aren't you going to begin, mummy?' said Rosalie at length.

'I almost wish I hadn't promised to tell you, child,' said her mother, hurriedly; 'it cuts me up so to think of it; but never mind; you ought to know, and you will know some day, so I'd better tell you myself. Rosalie, your mother was born a lady.

'Yes,' said the poor woman, as the child did not speak; 'I was never born to this life of misery; I brought myself to it. I chose it,' she said, bitterly; 'and I'm only getting the harvest of what I sowed myself.'

When she had said this, she turned deadly pale, and shivered from head to foot. Rosalie crept still closer to her, and put her little warm hand in her mother's cold one. Then the poor woman by a strong effort controlled herself, and she went on.

'So now, darling, I'll tell you all about it, just
as if I was talking about someone else; I'll forget
it is myself, or I shall never be able to tell it. I'll
try and fancy I'm on the stage, and talking about
the sorrows and troubles of someone I never knew,
and never cared for, and of whom I shall never
think again when my part is over.

'I was born in a country village, hundreds of
miles from here, in the south of England. My
father was the squire of the place. We lived in a
large mansion, which was built half-way up the
side of a wooded hill, and an avenue of beautiful
old trees led up to the house. There was a large
conservatory at one side of it filled with the rarest
flowers, and in a shady corner of the grounds my
mother had a kind of grotto, filled with lovely
ferns, through which a clear stream of water was
ever flowing. This fernery was my mother's great
delight, and here she spent much of her time. She
was a very worldly woman; she took very little
notice of her children; and when she was not in
the garden, she was generally lying on the sofa in
the drawing-room, reading novels which she procured from a London library.

'My father was a very different man; he was
fond of quiet, and fond of his children; but he was
obliged to be often from home, so that we did not
see as much of him as we should otherwise have
done.

'I had one brother and one sister. My brother
was much older than we were; there had been
several children between us, who had died in their
infancy, so that he was in the sixth form of a large

C

public school, while we were children in the nursery.

'My sister Lucy was a year younger than I was. She was such a pretty child, and had a very sweet disposition. When we were children we got on very well together, and shared every pleasure and every grief. My father bought us a little white pony; and on this we used to ride in turns about the park when we were quite small children, our old nurse following, to see that no harm came to us.

'She was a very good woman; she taught us to say our prayers night and morning, and on Sundays she used to sit with us under a tree in the park, and show us Scripture pictures, and tell us stories out of the Bible. There was one picture of a shepherd very like that, Rosalie; it came back to my mind the other day, when that old man gave it to you; only in mine the shepherd was just drawing the lamb out of a deep miry pit, into which it had fallen, and the text underneath it was this: "The Son of man is come to seek and to save that which is lost." We used to learn these texts and repeat them to our nurse when we looked at the pictures; and then, if we had said them correctly, she used to let us carry our tea into the park, and eat it under the tree. And after tea we used to sing one of our little hymns and say our prayers, and then she took us in and put us to bed. I have often thought of those quiet, happy Sundays when I have been listening to the noise and racket of the fair.

'I thought a great deal at the time about what our nurse told us. I remember one Sunday she had been reading to us about the Judgment Day. And that same afternoon there was a great thunderstorm; the lightning flashed in at the window, and the thunder rolled overhead. It made me think of what nurse had said about the Judgment Day. And then I knelt down, and **prayed** that God would take care. of me, and not let the lightning kill me. I crept behind the sofa in the large drawing-room, and trembled lest the books should be opened, and all my sins read out; and I asked God to keep them shut a little longer.

'I remember another day, when I had told a lie, but would not own that I had done so. Nurse would not let me sleep with Lucy, but moved my little bed into her room, that I might lie still, and think about my sin. It was a strange room, and I could not sleep for some time, but I lay awake with my eyes closed. When I opened them I saw one bright star shining in at the closed window. It seemed to me like the eye of God watching me; I could not get the thought out of my mind. I shut my eyes tightly that I might not see it; but I could not help opening them to see if it was still there. And when nurse came up to bed she found me weeping. I have often seen that star since, Rosalie, looking in at the window of the caravan; and it always reminds me of that night.

'I had a very strong will, Rosalie, and even as a child I hated to be controlled. If I set my heart on anything, I wanted to have it at once, and if I was opposed I was very angry. I loved my nurse; but when I was about eight years old she had to leave us to live with her mother, and then

I was completely unmanageable. My mother engaged a governess for us, who was to teach us in the morning and take us out in the afternoon. She was an indolent person, and she took very little trouble with us, and my mother did not exert herself sufficiently to look after us, or to see what we were doing. Thus we learnt very little and got into idle and careless habits. Our governess used to sit down in the park with a book, and we were allowed to follow our own devices, and amuse ourselves as we pleased.

'When my brother Gerald came home, it was always a great cause of excitement to us. We used to meet him at the station, and drive him home in triumph. Then we always had holidays, and Miss Manders went away, and Gerald used to amuse us with stories of his school friends, as we walked with him through the park. He was a very fine-looking lad, and my mother was very proud of him. She thought much more of him than of us, because he was a boy, and was to be the heir to the property. She liked to drive out with her handsome son, who was admired by every one who saw him, and sometimes we were allowed to go with them. We were generally left in the carriage, while mummy and Gerald called at the large houses of the neighbourhood; and we used to jump out, as soon as they had disappeared inside the house, and explore the different gardens, and plan how we would lay out our grounds when we had houses of our own. But what's that, Rosalie? —did the wagons stop?'

Rosalie ran to the door and looked out.

'Yes, mummy,' she said; 'my father's coming.'

'Then mind, not a word,' said her mother, in a hoarse whisper.

'Well!' said Augustus, entering the caravan in a theatrical manner, 'I thought I might as well enjoy the felicity of the amiable society of my lady and her daughter!'

This was said with a profound bow towards his wife and Rosalie.

'Glad to see you so much better, madam,' he continued. 'Rather singular, isn't it, that your health and spirits have revived immediately we have left the inspired scene of public action, or—to speak in plain terms—when there's no work to do?'

'I think it's the fresh air, Augustus, that has done me good; there was such a close, stifling smell from the fair, I felt worse directly we got there.'

'It's to be hoped,' he said, with a disagreeable smile on his face, 'that this resuscitation of the vital powers may be continued until we arrive at Lesborough; but the probability is that the moment we arrive on the scene of action you will be seized with that most unpleasant of all maladies, distaste to your work, and will be compelled once more to resume that most interesting and pathetic occupation of playing the invalid!'

'Oh! Augustus, don't speak to me like that!' said the poor wife.

Augustus made no answer, but taking a piece of paper from his pocket twisted it up, and putting it into the fire, lighted a long pipe and began to smoke. The fumes of the tobacco brought on his poor wife's cough, but he took very little notice of her, except to ask her occasionally, between the whiffs of his pipe, how long that melodious sound was to last. Then his eyes fell on Rosalie's picture, which was pinned to the side of the caravan.

'Where did you get that from?' he inquired, turning to his wife.

'It's mine, father,' said little Rosalie; 'an old gentleman in the fair gave it to me; isn't it pretty?'

'It will do for a child,' he said, scornfully. 'Toby, what are you after? You're creeping along; we shall never get there at this pace.'

'The horse is tired, master,' said Toby; 'he's had a long stretch these two days.'

'Beat him then,' said the cruel man; 'flog him well; do you think I can afford to waste time on the road? The wild beasts are a mile ahead, at the very least, and the marionettes will be there by this time. We shall just arrive when all the people have spent their money, and are tired out.'

Now there was one subject of standing dispute between Toby and his master. Toby was a kind-hearted lad and hated to see the horses over-worked, ill-fed, and badly used; he was always remonstrating with his master about it, and thereby bringing down on himself his master's wrath and abuse. Augustus cared nothing for the comfort or welfare of those under him. To get as much work as possible out of them, and to make as much gain by them as he could, was all he thought of. They might be tired, or hungry, or over-burdened; what did it matter to him, as long as the end for which he kept them was fulfilled? The same spirit which led him to treat his company and his wife with severity and indifference led him to ill-treat his horses.

Toby resolutely refused to beat the poor tired horse, which was already straining itself to its utmost, the additional weight of Augustus having been very trying to it the last few miles.

When Augustus saw that Toby did not mean to obey him, he sprang to the door of the caravan in a towering passion, seized the whip from Toby's hand, and then beat the poor horse unmercifully, causing it to start from side to side, till nearly everything in the caravan was thrown to the ground, and Rosalie and her mother trembled with suppressed indignation and horror.

With one last tremendous blow, aimed at Toby's head, Augustus threw down the whip, and returned to his pipe.

CHAPTER 5

ROSALIE'S FIRST SERMON

THE next morning, as soon as they had started on their journey, Rosalie begged her mother to continue her story. So, after satisfying herself that her husband did not intend to favour them with his company, the poor woman took up the thread of her story at the place at which she had left it when they were interrupted the day before.

'I was telling you, dear, about my life in that quiet country manor-house. I think I can remember nothing worth mentioning, until an event happened which altered the whole course of our lives.

'Lucy and I had been out riding in the park on the beautiful new horses which our father had given us a few months before. I can see Lucy now in her riding-habit—her fair hair hanging down her back, and her cheeks glowing with the air and exercise. She was very pretty, was my sister Lucy. People said I was handsomer than she was, and had a better figure and brighter eyes; but Lucy was a sweet-looking little thing, and no one could look at her without loving her.

'We got down from our horses, leaving them with the groom who had been riding out with us, and ran into the house. But we were met by one of the servants, with a face white with alarm, who begged us to go quietly upstairs, as our father was very ill, and the doctor said he was to be perfectly quiet. We asked her what was the matter with him, and she told us that as he had been riding home from the railway station, his horse, which was a young one he had just bought, had thrown him, and that he had been brought home insensible. More than this she could not tell us, but our mother came into our bedroom, and told us, with more feeling than I had ever seen in her face before, that our father could not live through the night.

'I shall never forget that night. It was the first time that I had been brought close to death, and it frightened me. I lay awake, listening to the hall clock as it struck one hour after another. Then I crept out of bed, and put my head out of the window. It was a close, oppressive night—not a breath seemed to be stirring. I wondered what was going on in the next room, and whether I should ever see my father again. Then I thought I heard a sound, but it was only Lucy sobbing beneath the bedclothes.'

'"Lucy," I said, glad to find she was awake, "isn't it a long night?"'

'"Yes, Norah," she answered; "I'm so frightened; shall we have a light?"'

'I found the matches and lighted a candle; but three or four large moths darted into the room, so that I had to close the window.

'We lay awake in our little beds watching the moths darting in and out of the candle, and straining our ears for any sound from our father's room. Each time a door shut we started, and sat up in bed listening.

'"Wouldn't you be frightened if you were dying, Norah?" said Lucy, under her breath.

'"Yes," I said, "I'm sure I should."

'Then there was silence again for a long time; and I thought Lucy had fallen asleep, when she got up in bed and spoke again:

'"Norah, do you think you would go to heaven if you were to die?"

'"Yes, of course," I said quickly; "why do you ask me?"

'"I don't think I should," said Lucy; "I'm almost sure I shouldn't."

'We lay still for about another hour, and then the door opened, and our mother came in. She was crying very much, and had a handkerchief to her eyes.

'"Your father wants to see you," she said; "come at once."

'We crept very quietly into the room of death, and stood beside our father's bed. His face was so altered that it frightened us, and we trembled from head to foot. But he held out his hand to us, Rosalie, and we drew closer to him. Then he whispered:

'"Good-bye! don't forget your father; and don't wait till you come to die to get ready for another world."

'Then we kissed him, and our mother told us to go back to bed. I never forgot my father's last words to us; and I often wondered what made him say them.

'The next morning we heard that our father was dead. Gerald arrived too late to see him; he was

at college then, and was just preparing for his
last examination.

'My mother seemed at first very much distressed
by my father's death; she shut herself up in her
room, and would see no one. The funeral was a
very grand one; all the people of the neighbourhood
came to it, and Lucy and I peeped out of one of
the top windows to see it start. After it was over
Gerald went back to college, and my mother
returned to her novels. I think she thought, Rosalie,
that she would be able to return to her old life much
as before. But no sooner had Gerald passed his
last examination than she received a letter from him
to say that he intended to be married in a few
months, and to bring his bride to the Hall. Then
for the first time the truth flashed on my mother's
mind, that she would soon be no longer the mistress
of the manor-house, but would have to seek a home
elsewhere. She seemed at first very angry with
Gerald for marrying so early; but she could say
nothing against his choice, for she was a young
woman of title, and one in every way suited to the
position she was to occupy.

'My mother at length decided to remove to a
town in the midland counties, where she would
have some good society and plenty of gaiety, as
soon as her mourning for my father was ended.

'It was a great trial to us, leaving the old home.
Lucy and I went round the park the day before
we left, gathering leaves from our favourite trees,
and taking a last look at the home of our childhood.
Then we walked through the house, and looked
out of the windows on the lovely wooded hills,

with eyes which were full of tears. I have never seen it since, and I shall never see it again. Sometimes, when we are coming through the country, it brings it back to my mind, and I could almost fancy I was walking down one of the long grassy terraces, or wandering in the quiet shade of the trees in the park. Hush! what was that, Rosalie?' said her mother, leaning forward to listen; 'was it music?'

At first Rosalie could hear nothing, except Toby whistling to his horse, and the rumbling of the wheels of the caravan. She went to the door and leaned out, and listened once more. The sun was beginning to set, for Rosalie's mother had only been able to talk at intervals during the day, from her frequent fits of coughing, and from numerous other interruptions, such as the preparations for dinner, the halting to give the horses rest, and the occasional visits of Augustus.

The rosy clouds were gathering in the west, as the pure evening breeze wafted to the little girl's ears the distant sound of bells.

'It's bells, mummy,' she said, turning round; 'church bells; can't you hear them? Ding-dong-bell, ding-dong-bell.'

'Yes,' said her mother, 'I can hear them clearly now; our nurse used to tell us they were saying, "Come and pray, come and pray." Oh! Rosalie, it is such a comfort to be able to speak of those days to someone! I've kept it all hidden up in my heart till sometimes I have felt as if it would burst!'

'I can see the church now, mummy,' said Rosalie; 'it's a pretty little grey church with a tower, and we're going through the village; aren't we, Toby?'

'Yes, Miss Rosie,' said Toby; 'we're going to stop there all night; the horses are tired out—even the master can see it now. We shall get on all the quicker for giving them a bit of rest.'

'Can't you hear the bells now, mummy?' said Rosalie, turning round.

'Yes,' said the poor woman; 'they sound just like the bells of our little church at home; I could almost cry when I hear them.'

By this time they had reached the village. It was growing dark, and the country people were lighting their candles, and gathering round their small fires. Rosalie could see inside many a cheerful little home, where the firelight was shining on the faces of the father, the mother and the children. How she wished they had a little home!

Ding-dong-bell, ding-dong-bell; still the chimes went on, and one and another came out of the small cottages, and took the road leading to the church, with their books under their arms.

Toby drove on; nearer and nearer the chimes sounded, until at last, just as the caravan reached a wide open common in front of the church, they ceased, and Rosalie saw the last old woman entering the church door before the service began. The wagons and caravans were drawn up on this open space for the night. Toby and the other men led the horses away to the stables of the inn; Augustus followed them, to enjoy himself among the lively company assembled in the little coffee-room, and Rosalie and her mother were left alone.

'Mummy dear,' said Rosalie, as soon as the men had turned the corner, 'may I go and peep at the church?'

'Yes, child,' said her mother; 'only don't make a noise if the people are inside.'

Rosalie did not wait for a second permission, but darted across the common, and opened the church gate. It was getting dark now, and the gravestones looked very solemn in the twilight. She went quickly past them, and crept along the side of the church to one of the windows. She could see inside the church quite well, because it was lighted up; but no one could see her as she was standing in the dark churchyard. Her bright quick eyes soon took in all that was to be seen. The minister was kneeling down, and so were all the people. There were a good many there, though the church was not full, as it was the week-evening service.

Rosalie watched at the window until all the people got up from their knees, when the clergyman gave out a hymn, and they began to sing. Rosalie then looked for the door, that she might hear the music better. It was a warm evening, and the door was open, and before she knew what she was about she had crept inside, and was sitting on a low seat just within. No one noticed her, for they were all looking in the opposite direction. Rosalie enjoyed the singing very much, and when it was over the clergyman began to speak. He had a clear, distinct voice, and he spoke in simple language which every one could understand.

Rosalie listened with all her might; it was the first sermon she had ever heard. 'The Son of man is come to seek and to save that which is lost.'

As soon as the service was over she stole out of the church and crept down the dark churchyard. She had passed through the little gate and was crossing the common to the caravan before the first person had left the church. To Rosalie's joy, her father had not returned; for he had found the society in the village inn extremely attractive. Rosalie's mother looked up as the child came in:

'Where have you been all this time, Rosalie?'

Rosalie gave an account of all she had seen, and told her how she had crept in at the open door of the church.

'What did the clergyman say, child?' asked her mother.

'He said your text, mummy—the text that was on your picture: "The Son of man is come to seek and to save that which is lost".'

'And what did he tell you about it?'

'He said Jesus went up and down looking for lost sheep, mummy; and he said we were all like sheep, and Jesus was looking for us. Do you think He is looking for you and me, mummy dear?'

'I don't know, child; I suppose so,' said her mother; '*I* shall take a great deal of looking for, I'm afraid.'

'But he said, mummy, that if only we would *let* Him find us, He would be sure to do it; He doesn't mind how much trouble He takes about it.'

Rosalie's mother was quite still for some time after this. Rosalie stood at the caravan door, watching the bright stars coming out one by one in the still sky.

'Mummy dear,' she said, 'is He up there?'

'Who, Rosalie, child?' said her mother.

'The Saviour; is He up in one of the stars?'

'Yes; heaven's somewhere there, Rosalie; up above the sky somewhere.'

'Would it be any good telling Him, mummy?

'Telling Him what, my dear?'

'Just telling Him that you and me want seeking and finding.'

'I don't know, Rosalie; you can try,' said her mother sadly.

'Please, Good Shepherd,' said Rosalie, looking up at the stars, 'come and seek me and mummy, and find us very quick, and carry us very safe, like the lamb in the picture.

'Will that do, mummy?' said Rosalie.

'Yes,' said her mother; 'I suppose so.'

Then Rosalie was still again, looking at the stars; but a sudden thought seized her.

'Mummy, ought I to have said amen?'

'Why, Rosalie?'

'I heard the people at church say it. Will it do any good without amen?'

'Oh, I don't think it matters much,' said her mother; 'you can say it now if you like.'

'Amen, amen,' said Rosalie, looking at the stars again.

Just then voices were heard in the distance, and Rosalie saw her father and the men crossing the dark common, and coming in the direction of the caravan.

CHAPTER 6

A FAMILY SECRET

How sweet and calm the village appeared the next morning, when Rosalie woke and looked out at it! She was quite sorry to leave it; but there was no rest for these poor wanderers, they must move onwards towards the town where they were next to perform. And, as they travelled on, Rosalie's mother went on with her sad story.

'I told you, darling, that my mother took a house in town, and that we all moved there, that my brother Gerald might take possession of our old home. We were getting big girls now, and my mother sent Miss Manders away, and left us to our own devices.

'My sister Lucy had been very different since our father died. She was so quiet and still, that I often wondered what was the matter with her. She spent nearly all her time reading her Bible in a little attic chamber. I did not know why she went there, till one day I went upstairs to get something out of a box, and found Lucy sitting in the window seat reading her little black Bible. I asked her what she read it for, and she said:

'"Oh, Norah! it makes me so happy; won't you come and read it with me?" But I tossed my head and said I had too much to do to waste my time like that; and I ran downstairs, and tried to forget what I had seen; for I knew that my sister was right and I was wrong. Oh, Rosalie, darling, I've often thought, if I had listened to my sister Lucy that day, what a different life I might have led!

'Well, I must go on; I'm coming to the saddest part of my story, and I had better get over it as quickly as I can.

'As I got older I took to reading novels. Our house was full of them, for my mother spent her days in devouring them. I read them and read them till I lived in them, and was never happy unless I was fancying myself one of the heroines of whom I read. My own life seemed dull and monotonous; I wanted to see more of the world, and to have something romantic happen to me. Oh, Rosalie, I got so restless and discontented! I used to wake in the night, and wonder what *my* fortunes would be; and then I used to light the candle and go on with the exciting novel I had been reading the night before. Often I used to read half the night, for I could not sleep again till I knew the end of the story. I quite left off saying my prayers, for I could not think of anything of that sort when I was in the middle of a novel.

'It was just about this time that I became acquainted with a family of the name of Roehunter. They were rich people, friends of my mother. Miss Georgina and Miss Laura Roehunter were very fast, dashing girls. They took a great fancy to me, and we were always together. They were passionately fond of the theatre, and they took me to it night after night.

'I could think of nothing else, Rosalie. I dreamt of it every night. It took even more hold of me than the novels had done, for it seemed to me like a *living* novel. I admired the scenery; I admired the actors; I admired everything that I saw. I thought if I was only on the stage I should be perfectly happy. There was nothing in the world that I wanted so much; it seemed to me such a free, happy, romantic life. When an actress was greeted with bursts of applause, I almost envied her. How wearisome my life seemed when compared with hers!

'I kept a diary then, Rosalie darling, in which I wrote all that I did every day, and I used to write again and again:

'"No change yet; my life wants variety; it is the same over and over again."

'I determined that as soon as possible I would have a change, cost what it might.

'Soon after this the Roehunters told me that they were going to have some private theatricals, and that I must come and help them. It was just what I wanted. Now, I thought, I could fancy myself an actress.

'They engaged some of the professional actors at the theatre to teach us our parts, to arrange the scenery, and to help us to do everything in the best possible manner. I had to go up to the Roehunters' again and again to learn my part of the performance. And there it was, Rosalie dear, that I met your father. He was one of the actors whom they employed.

'You can guess what came next, my darling. Your father saw how well I could act, and how passionately fond I was of it; and by degrees he found out how much I should like to do it always, instead of leading my humdrum life at home. So he used to meet me in the street, and talk to me about it, and he told me that if I would only come with him, I should have a life of pleasure and excitement, and never know what care was. And he arranged that the day after these private theatricals we should run away and be married.

'Oh, darling! I shall never forget that day. I arrived home late at night, or rather early in the morning, worn out with the evening's entertainment. I had been much praised for the way I had performed my part, and some of the company had declared I should make a first-rate actress, and I thought to myself that they little knew how soon I was to become one. As I drove home, I felt in a perfect whirl of excitement. The day had come at last. Was I glad? I hardly knew; I tried to think I was; but somehow I felt sick at heart; I could not shake that feeling off, and as I walked upstairs I felt perfectly miserable.

'My mother had gone to bed; and I never saw her again! Lucy was fast asleep, lying with her hand under her cheek, sleeping peacefully. I stood a minute or two looking at her. Her little Bible was lying beside her, for she had been reading it the last thing before she went to sleep. Oh, Rosalie! I would have given anything to change places with Lucy then. But it was too late now; Augustus was to meet me outside the house, and we were to be married at a church in the town that very morning. Our names had been posted up in the registry office some weeks before.

'I turned away from Lucy, and began putting some things together to take with me, and I hid them under the bed lest Lucy should wake and see them. It was no use going to bed, for I had not got home from the theatricals till three o'clock, and in two hours Augustus would come. So I scribbled a little note to my mother, telling her that when she received it I should be married, and that I would call and see her in a few days. Then I put out the light, lest it should wake my sister, and sat waiting in the dark. And, Rosie dear, that star—the same star that I had seen that night when I was a little girl, and had told that lie— that same star came and looked in at the window. And it seemed to me like the eye of God.

'I felt so frightened, that once I thought I would not go; I almost determined to write Augustus a note giving it up; but I thought that he would laugh at me for being such a coward, and I tried to picture to myself once more how fine it would be to be a real actress, and be always praised as I had been last night.

'Then I got up, and drew down the blind, that I might hide the star from sight. I was so glad to see it beginning to get light, for I knew that the star would fade away, and that Augustus would soon come.

'At last the church clock struck five, so I took my bag from under the bed, wrapped myself up in a warm shawl, and leaving my note on the dressing-table, prepared to go downstairs. But I turned back when I got to the door, to look once more at my sister Lucy. And, Rosalie darling, as

I looked I felt as if my tears would choke me. I wiped them hastily away, however, and crept downstairs. Every creaking board made me jump and tremble lest I should be discovered, and at every turning I expected to see some one watching me. But no one appeared: I got down safely, and, cautiously unbolting the hall-door, I stole quietly out into the street, and soon found Augustus, who carried my bag. That morning we were married.

'Then my troubles began. It was not half as pleasant being an actress as I had thought it would be. I knew nothing then of the life behind the scenes. I did not know how tired I should be, nor what a comfortless life I should lead.

'Oh, Rosalie! I was soon sick of it. I would have given worlds to be back in my old home. I would have given worlds to lead that quiet, peaceful life again. I was much praised and applauded in the theatre; but after a time I cared very little for it; and as for the acting itself, I became thoroughly sick of it. I have often and often fallen asleep, unable to undress myself from weariness after acting in the play; and again and again I have wished that I had never seen the inside of a theatre, and never known anything of the wretched life of an actress!

'We stopped for some time in the town where my mother lived, for Augustus had an engagement in a theatre there, and he procured one for me. We had miserable lodgings, and often were very badly off. I called at home a few days after I was married; but the servant shut the door in my face, saying that my mother never wished to see me again, or to hear my name mentioned. I used to walk up and down outside, trying to catch a glimpse of my sister Lucy; but she was never allowed to go out alone, and I could not get an opportunity of speaking to her. All my old friends passed me in the street—even the Roehunters would take no notice of me whatever.

'Then your father lost his engagement at the theatre—I need not tell you why, Rosalie darling—and we left the town. And then I began to know what poverty meant. We travelled from place to place, sometimes getting occasional jobs at small town theatres, sometimes stopping at a town for a few months, and then being dismissed, and travelling on for weeks without hearing of any employment.

'It was then that your little brother was born. Such a pretty baby he was, and I named him Arthur, after my father. I was very, very poor when he was born, and I could hardly get clothes for him to wear, but oh, Rosalie darling, I loved him very much. I wrote to my mother to tell her about it, and that baby was to be christened after my father; but she sent back my letter unread, and I never wrote to her again. And one day, when I took up a newspaper, I saw my mother's death in it; and I heard afterwards that she said on her dying bed that I was not to be told of her death till she was put under the ground, for I had been a disgrace and a shame to the family. And that, they said, was the only time that she mentioned me, after the week that I ran away.

'My sister Lucy wrote me a very kind letter after my mother died, and sent me some presents; but

I was sorry for it afterwards, for your father kept writing to her for money, and telling her long tales about the distress I was in, to make her send us more.

'She often sent us money; but I felt as if I could not bear to take it. And she used to write me such beautiful letters—to beg me to come to Jesus, and to remember what my father had said to us when he died. She said Jesus had made *her* happy, and would make me happy too. I often think now of what she said, Rosalie.

'Well, after a time I heard that Lucy was married to a clergyman, and your father heard it too, and he kept writing to her and asking her for money again and again. And at last came a letter from her husband, in which he said that he was very sorry to be obliged to tell us that his wife could do no more for us; and he requested that no more letters on the same subject might be addressed to her, as they would receive no reply.

'Your father wrote again; but they did not answer, and since then they have left the town where they were living, and he lost all clue to them. And, Rosalie darling, I hope he will never find them again. I cannot bear to be an annoyance to my sister Lucy—my dear little sister Lucy.

'As for Gerald, he has taken no notice of us at all. Your father has written to him from time to time, but his letters have always been returned to him.

'Well, so we went on, getting poorer and poorer. Once your father took a situation as a postmaster in a small country village, and there was a woman there who was very kind to me. She used to come and see my little Arthur: he was very delicate, and at last he took a dreadful cold, it settled on his chest, and my poor little lamb died. And, Rosalie darling, when I buried him under a little willow-tree in that country churchyard, I felt as if I had nothing left to live for.

'We did not stay in that village long; we were neither of us used to keeping accounts, and we got them in a complete muddle. So I had to leave behind my little grave, and the only home we ever had.

'Then your father fell in with a strolling actor, who was in the habit of frequenting fairs, and between them, by selling their furniture, and almost everything they possessed, they bought some scenery and a caravan, and started a travelling theatre. And, when the man died, Rosalie, he left his share of it to your father.

'So the last twelve years, my darling, I've been moving about from place to place, just as we are doing now. And in this caravan, my little girl, you were born. I was very ill a long time after that, and could not take my place in the theatre, and, for many reasons, that was the most miserable part of my miserable life.

'Now, little woman, I have told you all I need tell you at present; perhaps some day I can give you more particulars; but you will have some idea now why I am so utterly wretched.

'Yes, utterly wretched!' said the poor woman; 'no hope for this world, and no hope for the next.'

'Poor, poor mummy!' said little Rosalie, stroking

her hand very gently and tenderly, 'poor mummy dear!'

'It's all my own fault, child,' said her mother; 'I've brought it all on myself, and I've no one but myself to blame.'

'Poor, poor mummy!' said Rosalie again.

Then the sick woman seemed quite exhausted, and lay on her bed for some time without speaking or moving. Rosalie sat by the door of the caravan, and sang softly to herself:

> 'Jesus, I Thy face am seeking,
> Early will I come to Thee.'

'Oh, Rosalie!' said her mother, looking round, 'I didn't come to Him early; oh, if I only had! Mind you do, Rosie; it's so much easier for you now than when you get to be old and wicked like me.'

'Is that what "In the sunshine of the morning" means, in the next verse, mummy dear?'

'Yes, Rosalie,' said her mother; 'it means when you're young and happy. Oh, dear, dear! if I'd only come to Him then!'

'Why don't you come now, mummy dear?'

'I don't know; I don't expect He would take me now; I have been such a sinner! There are other things, child, I have not told you about; and they are all coming back to my mind now. I don't know how it is, Rosalie, I never thought so much of them before.'

'Perhaps the Good Shepherd is beginning to find you, mummy.'

'I don't know, Rosalie! I wish I could think that. Anyhow, they are all rising up as clear as if I saw them all; some of them are things I did years and years ago, even when I was a little girl in that old home in the country; they are all coming back to me now, and oh! I am so very, very miserable.'

'Rosalie,' said her father's voice, at the door of the caravan, 'come into the next wagon. We've a new play on at this town, and you have your part to learn. Come away!'

Rosalie had to leave her poor mother; and instead of singing the soothing words of the hymn, she had to repeat again and again the foolish and senseless words which had fallen to her share in the new play which her father was getting up. Over and over again she repeated them, till she was weary of their very sound, her father scolding her if she made a mistake, or failed to give each word its proper emphasis. And when she was released it was time to get tea ready; and then they halted for the night at a small market town, just eight miles from Lesborough, where they were next to perform, and which they were to enter the next morning, as the fair began on Monday.

CHAPTER 7

THE CIRCUS PROCESSION

It was a bright, sunny morning when the theatre party reached Lesborough. Not a cloud was to be seen in the sky, and Augustus was in capital spirits, for he thought that if the fine weather lasted his profits would be larger than usual.

On the road leading to the town they passed several small shows bound for the same destination. There was the show of 'The Lancashire Lass,' 'The Exhibition of the Performing Little Pigs,' 'Roderick Polglaze's Living Curiosities,' and 'The Show of the Giant Horse.' Augustus knew the proprietor of nearly every caravan that passed them, and they exchanged greetings by the way, and congratulated each other on the fine weather which seemed to be before them.

Then they drew near the town, and heard a tremendous noise in the distance. As they entered the main street they saw a cloud of dust in front of them, and then an immense crowd of people. Rosalie and her mother came to the door of the caravan and looked out.

Presently the dust cleared away, and showed them a glittering gilded car, which was coming towards them, surrounded by throngs of boys and girls, men and women.

'What is it, Toby?' asked Rosalie.

'It's a large circus, Miss Rosie; master said they were going to be here, and he was afraid they would carry a good many people off from us.'

The theatre party had to draw up on one side of the street to let the long procession pass.

First came a gilded car filled with musicians, who were playing a noisy tune. This was followed by about a dozen men on horseback, some dressed in shining armour, as knights of the olden time, and others as cavaliers of the time of the Stuarts.

Then came another large gilded car, on the top of which was a golden dragon, with coloured reins round its neck, which were held by an old man, dressed as an ancient Briton, and supposed to personate St. George. Then came a number of mounted women, dressed in brilliant velvet habits, one green, one red, one yellow, one violet; each of them holding long orange reins, which were fastened to spirited piebald horses, which they drove before them.

These were followed by a man riding on two ponies, standing with one leg on each, and going at a great pace. Then two little girls and a little boy passed on three diminutive ponies, and next a tiny carriage, drawn by four little cream-coloured horses, and driven by a boy dressed as the Lord Mayor's coachman.

After these came an absurd succession of clowns, driving, riding, or standing on donkeys, and dressed in hideous costumes. Then, three or four very tall and fine horses led by grooms in scarlet.

Lastly, an enormous gilded car, drawn by six piebald horses, with coloured flags on their heads.

On the top of this car sat a girl, intended for Britannia, dressed in white, with a scarlet scarf across her shoulders, a helmet on her head, and a trident in her hand. She was leaning against two large shields, which alone prevented her from falling from her giddy height. Some way below her, in front of the car, sat her two maidens, dressed in glittering silver tinsel, on which the rays of the sun made it dazzling to look: while behind her, clinging on to the back of the car, were two iron-clad men, whose scaly armour was also shining brightly.

The procession over, there was nothing to be heard or seen but a noisy rabble hastening on to get another glimpse of the wonderful sight.

Some girls were standing near the caravan close to Rosalie and her mother, as the circus procession passed, and they were perfectly enraptured with all they saw. When Britannia came in sight they could hardly contain themselves, so envious were they. One of them told the other she would give anything to be sitting up there, dressed in gold and silver, and she thought Britannia must be as happy as Queen Victoria.

'Oh!' said Rosalie's mother, leaning out and speaking in a low voice, 'you would *soon* get tired of it.'

'Not I,' said the girl; 'I only wish I had the chance.'

Rosalie's mother sighed, and said to Rosalie, 'Poor things! they little know; I should not wonder if that poor girl is about as wretched as I am. But people don't consider; they know nothing about it; they have to be behind the scenes to know what it is like.'

Nothing further happened until the theatre party reached the place where the fair was to be held. It was a large open square in the middle of the town, which was generally used as a market-place. Although it was only Saturday morning, and the fair was not to begin until Monday, many of the shows had already arrived. The marionettes and the wild-beast show had completed their arrangements, and one of the roundabouts was already in action, and from time to time its proprietor rang a large bell, to call together a fresh company of riders.

The children had a holiday, as it was Saturday, and they rushed home and clamoured for pennies, that they might spend them in sitting on a wooden horse, or elephant, or camel, or in one of the small omnibuses or open carriages, and then being taken round by means of steam at a tremendous pace, till their breath was nearly gone; and when they alighted once more on the ground, they hardly knew where they were, or whether they were standing on their heads or on their feet. And for long after many of these children were dizzy and sick, and felt as if they were walking on ground which gave way beneath them as they trod on it.

As soon as Augustus arrived at the place where his theatre was to be erected, he and his men began their work. For the next few hours there was nothing to be heard on all sides but rapping and hammering, every one working with all his might to get everything finished before sunset. Each half-hour fresh shows arrived, had their ground measured out for them by the market-keeper, and began to unload and fasten up immediately.

Rosalie stood at the door and looked out; but she had seen it all so often before that it was no amusement to her, and she felt very glad as, one by one, the shows were finished and the hammering ceased.

Just as she hoped that all was becoming quiet, she heard a dreadful noise at the back of the caravan. It was her father's voice, and he was in a towering passion with one of the men, who had annoyed him by neglecting to put up part of the scaffolding properly. The two men shouted at each other for some time, and a large number of people, who were strolling about among the shows, collected round them to see what was the matter.

At length a policeman, seeing the crowd, came and ordered them off, and they were obliged to retreat inside the theatre.

That night Augustus came into the caravan to smoke his pipe, and informed his wife that it was very well she was so much better, for he and Conrad had disagreed, and Conrad had taken his things and gone off, so of course she would have to take her part on Monday night.

Rosalie looked at her mother, and Rosalie's mother looked at her, but neither of them spoke.

As soon as her father had left them for the night, Rosalie said:

'Mummy dear, you'll *never* be able to stand all that long, long time; I'm sure it will make you worse, mummy dear.'

'Never mind, Rosalie; it's no use telling your father; he thinks I am only complaining if I do.'

'But oh, mummy dear, what if it makes you bad again, as it did before?'

'It can't be helped, child; I shall have to do it, so it's no use talking about it; I may as well do it without making a fuss about it; your father is put out to-night, darling, and it would never do to annoy him more.'

Little Rosalie was not satisfied; she looked very tenderly and sorrowfully at her mother; and the next morning she went timidly to tell her father that she did not think her mother would ever get through her part, she was too weak for it. But he told her shortly to mind her own business; so little Rosalie could do nothing more—nothing, except watch her mother very carefully and gently all that long, dreary Sunday, scarcely allowing her to rise from her seat, but fetching her everything she wanted, and looking forward sick at heart to the morrow.

The church-bells chimed in all directions; crowds of people passed along the market-place to church or chapel; but to Rosalie and her mother Sunday brought no joy.

It was a fine, bright day, so most of the show-people were roaming about the town; but Rosalie's mother was too weak to go out, and her little girl did not like to leave her.

'Rosalie,' said her mother, that Sunday afternoon, 'I'm going to give you a present.'

'A present for me, mummy dear!' said Rosalie.

E

'Yes, little woman; pull that large box from under the bed. It's rather heavy, dear; can you manage it?'

'Oh yes, mummy dear, quite well.'

Rosalie's mother sat down by the box, and began to unpack it. At the top of the box were some of her clothes and Rosalie's; but it was a long time since she had turned out the things at the bottom of the box. She took out from it a small bundle pinned up in a towel, then, calling Rosalie to her side, she drew out the pins one by one, and opened it. Inside were several small parcels carefully tied up in paper.

In the first parcel was a little pair of blue shoes, with a tiny red sock.

'Those were my little Arthur's, Rosalie,' said her mother, with tears in her eyes; 'I put them away the day he was buried, and I've never liked to part with them. No one will care for them when I'm gone, though,' said she, with a sigh.

'Oh, mummy dear,' said Rosalie, 'don't talk so!'

The next parcel contained a small square box; but before Rosalie's mother opened it she went to the door and looked cautiously out. Then, after seeing that no one was near, she touched a spring, and took out of the velvet-lined case a beautiful little locket. There was a circle of pearls all round it, and the letters 'N. E. H.' were engraved in a monogram outside.

Then she opened the locket, and showed Rosalie the picture of a girl with a very sweet and gentle face, and large, soft brown eyes.

'Rosalie, darling,' said her mother, 'that is my sister Lucy.'

Rosalie took the locket in her hand, and looked at it very earnestly.

'Yes,' said the poor woman, 'that is my sister Lucy—my own sister Lucy. I haven't looked at it for many a day; I can hardly bear to look at it now, for I shall never see her again—never, darling! What's that, Rosalie?' she said, fearfully, covering the locket with her apron, as someone passed the caravan.

'It's only some men strolling through the fair, mummy dear,' said Rosalie.

'Because I wouldn't have your father see this for the world; he would soon sell it if he did. I've hid it all these years, and never let him find it. I could not bear to part with it; she gave it to me on my last birthday that I was at home. I remember it so well, Rosalie dear; I had been very disagreeable to Lucy a long time before that, for I knew I was doing wrong, and I had such a weight on my mind that I could not shake it off, and it made me cross and irritable.

'Lucy was never cross with me; she always spoke gently and kindly to me; and I sometimes even wished she would be angry, that I might have some excuse for my bad behaviour.

'Well, dear, when I woke that morning I found this little box laid on my pillow, and a note with it, asking me to accept this little gift from my sister Lucy, and always to keep it for her sake. Oh, Rosalie darling, wasn't it good of her when I had been so bad to her?

'Well, I kissed her, and thanked her for it, and I wore it round my neck; and when I ran away that morning I put it safely in my bag, and I've kept it ever since. Your father has not seen it for many years, and he has forgotten all about it. When we were so poor, I used to be so afraid he would remember this locket and sell it, as he did all my other jewels. It was hard enough parting with some of them; but I did not care so much as long as I kept this one, for I promised Lucy that morning that I would *never, never* part with it.'

'It is pretty, mummy dear,' said Rosalie.

'Yes, child; it will be yours some day, when I die; remember, it is for you; but you must never let it be sold or pawned, Rosalie; I couldn't bear to think it ever would be. And now we'll put it back again; it won't be safe here; your father might come in any minute.'

'Here's one more parcel, mummy.'

'Yes, keep that out, dear; that's your present,' said her mother. 'I can't give you the locket yet, because I must keep it till I die; but you shall have the other to-day.'

She took off the paper, and put into Rosalie's hands a small Testament. The child opened the book, and read on the fly-leaf, 'Mrs. Augustus Joyce. From her friend Mrs. Bernard, in remembrance of little Arthur, and with the prayer that she may meet her child in heaven.'

'I promised her that I would read it, Rosalie; but I haven't,' said the poor woman; 'I read a few verses the first week she gave it to me; but

I've never read it since. I wish I had—oh, I *do* wish I had!'

'Let me read it to you, mummy dear.'

'That's what I got it out for, darling; you might read a bit of it to me every day; I don't know whether it will do me any good; it's almost too late now; but I can but try.'

'Shall I begin at once, mummy dear?'

'Yes, directly, Rosalie; I'll just write your name in it, that you may always remember your mother when you see it.'

Rosalie brought her a pen and ink, and she wrote at the bottom of the page—'My little Rosalie, with her mother's love.'

'And now, child, you may begin to read.'

'What shall it be, mummy dear?'

'Find the part about your picture, dear; I should think it will say under the text where it is.'

With some trouble Rosalie found Luke xv and began to read:

'And He spake this parable unto them, saying, What man of you, having an hundred sheep, if he lose one of them, doth not leave the ninety and nine in the wilderness, and go after that which is lost, until he find it? And when he hath found it, he layeth it on his shoulders, rejoicing. And when he cometh home, he calleth together his friends and neighbours, saying unto them, Rejoice with me, for I have found my sheep which was lost. I say unto you, that likewise joy shall be in heaven over one sinner that repenteth, more than over ninety and nine just persons which need no repentance.'

'*I* need repentance, Rosalie, child,' said her mother.

'What is repentance, mummy dear?'

'It means being sorry for what you've done, Rosalie darling, and hating yourself for it, and wishing never to do wrong again.'

'Then, mummy, if you need repentance, you must be like the *one* sheep, not like the ninety-nine.'

'Yes, child, I'm a lost sheep; there's no doubt about that; I've gone very far astray—so far that I don't suppose I shall ever get back again; it's much easier to get wrong than to get right; it's a *very*, *very* hard thing to find the right road when you've once missed it; it doesn't seem much use my trying to get back; I have such a long way to go.'

'But, mummy dear, isn't it just like the sheep?'

'What do you mean, Rosalie darling?'

'Why, the sheep couldn't find its way back, could it, mummy? sheep never can find their way. And this sheep didn't walk back; did it? He carried it on his shoulder, like my picture; I don't suppose it would seem so very far when he carried it.'

Rosalie's mother made no answer when her child said this; but she seemed to be thinking about it. She sat looking thoughtfully out of the window: much, very much was passing through her mind. Then Rosalie closed the Testament, and wrapping it carefully in the paper in which it had been kept so many years, she hid it away in the box again.

It was Sunday evening now, and once more the church-bells rang, and once more the people went past with books in their hands. Rosalie wished very much that she could creep into one of the churches and hear another sermon. But just then her father and the men came back and wanted their tea; and, instead of the quiet service, Rosalie had to listen to their loud talking and noisy laughter.

Then her father sent for her into the large caravan, and made her go through her part of the play. She was just finishing her recital as the people passed back again from evening service.

CHAPTER 8

LITTLE MOTHER MANIKIN

IT was Monday night, and Rosalie's mother was dressing herself, to be ready to act in the play. Rosalie was standing beside her, setting out the folds of her white dress, and fetching everything she needed: her large necklace of pearl beads, the wreath of white lilies for her hair, and the bracelets, rings, and other articles of mock jewellery with which she was adorned. All these Rosalie brought to her, and the poor woman put them on one by one, standing before the tiny looking-glass to arrange them in their proper places.

It was a very thin, sorrowful face which that glass reflected; so ill and careworn, so weary and sad. As soon as she was ready she sat down on one of the boxes while Rosalie dressed herself.

'Oh, mummy dear,' said Rosalie, 'I'm sure you are not fit to act to-night.'

'Hush, Rosalie!' said her mother; 'don't speak of that now: come and sit beside me, darling, and let me do your hair for you; and before we go, Rosalie dear, sing your little hymn.'

Rosalie tried to sing it; but, somehow, her voice trembled, and she could not sing it very steadily. There was such a sad expression in her mother's face that, in the middle of the hymn, little Rosalie burst into tears, and threw her arms round her mother's neck.

'Don't cry, darling, don't cry!' said her mother; 'what is the matter with you, Rosalie?'

'Oh, mummy dear, I don't want you to go to-night!'

'Hush, little one!' said her mother; 'don't speak of that; listen to me, dear; I want you to make your mother a promise to-night; I want you to promise me that, if ever you can escape from this life of misery, you will do so; it's not good for you, darling, all this wretched acting—and oh! it makes my heart ache every time you have to go to it. You'll leave it if you can, Rosalie; won't you?'

'Yes, mummy dear, if you'll come with me,' said little Rosalie.

The poor mother shook her head sorrowfully.

'No, dear; I shall never leave the caravan now. I chose this life myself; I chose to live here, darling; and here I shall have to die. But you didn't choose it, child; and I pray that God may save you from it. You remember that little village we passed through, where you got your card?'

'Yes, mummy dear—where we had the milk and bread.'

'Do you remember a house which I sent you to look at?'

'Oh, yes, mummy dear—the house with a pretty garden, and a woman and her little girl gathering roses.'

'That woman was my sister Lucy, Rosalie.'

'Aunt Lucy!' said Rosalie; 'was it, mummy dear? And was that little girl my cousin?'

'Yes, darling; I knew it was your aunt Lucy as soon as that young woman mentioned her name.

Lucy married a Mr. Leslie; and it was just like her to read to those people in the cottages, just as she used to do when we lived in that town of which I told you.'

'Then I've really seen her?' said Rosalie.

'Yes, darling; and now I want you to promise me that, if ever you have the opportunity of getting to your aunt Lucy without your father knowing it, you'll go. I've written a letter to her, dear, and I've hid it away in that box, inside the case where the locket is. And if ever you can go to your aunt Lucy, give her that letter; you will, won't you, Rosalie? and show her that locket; she will remember it as soon as she sees it; and tell her, darling, that I never, never parted with it all these long, dreary years.'

'Why won't you come with me, mummy dear?'

'Don't ask me that now, darling; it's nearly time for us to go into the theatre. But before you go, just read those verses about your picture once through; we shall just about have time for it before your father comes.'

So Rosalie read once more the parable of the Lost Sheep.

'Rosalie, child,' said her mother, when she had finished, 'there are four words in that story which I've had in my mind, oh! so many times, since you read it last.'

'What are they, mummy dear?'

'"Until he find it," Rosalie. All last night I lay awake coughing, and I kept thinking there was no hope for me; it was no use my asking the Good Shepherd to look for me. But all of a sudden those words came back to me just as if someone had said them to me. "Until he find it—until he find it. He goeth after that which is lost until he find it. It seems He doesn't give up at once, He goes on looking until He finds it. And then it seemed to me, Rosalie—I don't know if I was right, I don't know if I even dare hope it, but it seemed to me last night that perhaps, if He takes such pains and looks so long—if He goes on *until He finds it*—there might even be a chance for me.'

'Are you ready?' said Augustus' voice, at the door of the caravan; 'we're just going to begin.'

Rosalie and her mother jumped up hastily, and, thrusting the Testament into the box, they hurried down the caravan steps and went into the theatre. There were still a few minutes before the performance commenced; and Rosalie made her mother sit down on a chair in the little room behind the stage, that she might rest as long as possible.

Several of the company came up to the poor woman, and asked her how she was, in tones which spoke of rough though kindly sympathy. Rosalie looked earnestly in their faces, and read there that they did not think her mother equal to her work; and it filled her little heart with sorrowful forebodings.

She had never seen her mother look more lovely than she did at the beginning of the play; there was a bright colour in her face, and her beautiful eyes shone more brilliantly than ever before. Rosalie really hoped she must be better, to look as well as that. But there was a weary, sorrowful expression in her face, which went to the child's heart. Her mother repeated the words of the play as if they were extremely distasteful to her, and as if she could hardly bear the sound of her own voice. In her eyes there was a wistful yearning, as if she were looking at and longing for something far, far away from the noisy theatre. She never smiled at the bursts of applause; she repeated her part almost mechanically, and, from time to time, Rosalie saw her mother's eyes fill with tears. She crept to her side, and put her little hand in hers as they went up to the platform after the first performance was over.

Her mother's hand was burning with fever, and yet she shivered from head to foot as they went out on the platform into the chill night air.

'Oh, mummy dear,' said Rosalie, in a whisper, 'you ought to go back to the caravan now.'

Rosalie's mother shook her head mournfully.

About half-way through the next play there came a long piece which Rosalie had to recite alone, the piece which her father had been teaching her during the last week. She was just half-way through it, when, suddenly, her eyes fell on her mother, who was standing at the opposite side of the stage in a tragical position. All the colour had gone from her face, and it seemed to Rosalie that each moment her face was growing whiter and more death-like. She quite forgot the words she was saying, all remembrance of them faded from her mind. She came to a sudden stop. Her father's promptings were all in vain, she could hear nothing he said, she could see nothing but her mother's sorrowful and ghastly face.

Then her mother fell, and some of the actors carried her from the room. Rosalie rushed forward to follow her, and the noise in the theatre became deafening. But she was stopped on the stairs by her father, who blamed her most cruelly for breaking down in her part, and ordered her to return immediately and finish, accompanying his command with most awful threatenings if she refused to obey.

Poor little Rosalie went on with her recital, trembling in every limb. Her mother's place was taken by another actor, and the play proceeded as before. But Rosalie's heart was not there. It was filled with a terrible, sickening dread. What had become of her mother? Who was with her? Were they taking care of her? And then a horrible fear came over her lest her mother should be dead —lest when she went into the caravan again she should only see her mother's body stretched on the bed—lest she should never, never hear her mother speak to her again.

As soon as the play was over, she went up to her father, and, in spite of the annoyed expression of his face, begged him to allow her to leave the theatre and to go to her mother. But he told her angrily that she had spoilt his profits quite enough for one night, and she must take care how she dared to do so again.

Oh! what a long night that seemed to Rosalie! When they went out on the platform between the performances, she gazed earnestly in the direction of her mother's caravan. A light seemed to be burning inside, but more than that Rosalie could not see.

It appeared as if the long hours would never pass away. Each time she went through her recital she felt glad that she had at least once less to say it. Each time that the Town-hall clock struck she counted the hours before the theatre would close. And yet, when all was over, and when Rosalie was at length allowed to return to the caravan, she hardly dared to enter it. What would she find within? Was her mother dead, and was her father hiding it from her till her part was over, lest she should break down again?

Very, very gently she opened the door. There was a candle burning on the table, and by its light Rosalie could see her mother lying on the bed. She was very pale, and her eyes were tightly closed. But she was breathing, she was not dead. The relief was so great that Rosalie burst into tears.

When she first came into the caravan she thought that her mother was alone, but a small hoarse whisper came from the corner of the caravan:

'Don't be frightened, my dear!' said the voice; 'it's only me. Toby told me about your mother, and so I came to sit with her till you came.'

Rosalie walked to her mother's side, and on the box by the bed she found a little creature about three feet high, with a very old and wrinkled face.

'Who are you?' said Rosalie.

'I belong to the Dwarf Show, my dear,' said the old woman, 'there are four of us there, and not one of us more than three feet high.'

'Isn't it going on to-night?' said Rosalie.

'Yes, it's going on, my dear; it always goes on,'

said the tiny old woman; 'but I'm old and ugly, you see, so I can be better spared than the others, I only go in sometimes, my dear; old age must have its liberties, you see.'

'Thank you so much for taking care of my mother,' said Rosalie; 'has she spoken to you yet?'

'Yes, my dear,' said the old woman; 'she spoke once, but I couldn't well hear what she said. I tried to reach up near to her mouth to listen; but you see I'm only three feet high, so I couldn't quite manage it. I thought it was something about a sheep, but of course it couldn't be that, my dear; there are no sheep here!'

'Oh, yes!' said Rosalie; 'that would be it; we had been reading about sheep before we went into the theatre.'

Just then a noise was heard at the door of the caravan, and Augustus entered. He went up to his wife, and felt her pulse; then he muttered:

'She's all right now; let her have a good sleep, that's all she wants, Rosalie.'

He looked curiously at the dwarf, and then left the caravan and shut the door.

'Rosalie,' said the tiny old woman when he had gone, 'I'll stop with you to-night if you like.'

'Oh! would you?' said little Rosalie; 'I should be so glad.'

She felt as if she could not bear all those long, dark hours alone, beside her unconscious mother.

'Yes,' said the dwarf; 'I'll stay; only you must go and tell them in our tent. Can you find it, do you think?'

'Where is it?' said Rosalie.

The little old woman described the situation of the tent, and Rosalie put a shawl over her head, and went in search of it. There were some stalls still lighted, and these showed Rosalie an immense picture hanging over the tent, representing a number of diminutive men and women; and above the picture there was a board, on which was written in large letters—'The Royal Show of Dwarfs.'

Rosalie had some difficulty in finding the entrance to this show. She groped round it several times, pulling at the canvas in different places, but all to no purpose. Then she heard voices within, laughing and talking. Going as near to these as possible, she put her mouth to a hole in the canvas, and called out:

'Please will you let me in? I've brought a message from the little woman that lives here.'

There was a great shuffling in the tent after this, and a clinking of money; then a piece of the canvas was pulled aside, and a little squeaky voice called out:

'Come in, whoever you are, and let us hear what you've got to say.'

Rosalie crept in through the canvas, and stepped into the middle of the tent.

It was a curious scene which she saw when she looked round. Three little dwarfs stood before her, dressed in the most extraordinary costumes, and far above over their heads there towered a tall and very thin giant. Not one of the tiny dwarfs came up to his elbow. On the floor were scattered tiny tables, diminutive chairs, and dolls' umbrellas, which the little people had been using in their performance.

'What is it, my dear?' said the giant, loftily, as Rosalie entered.

'Please,' said Rosalie, 'I've brought a message from the little woman that belongs to this show.'

'Mother Manikin,' said one of the dwarfs, in an explanatory tone.

'Yes, Mother Manikin,' repeated the giant; and the two other dwarfs nodded their heads in assent.

'My mother's very ill,' said Rosalie; 'and she's taking care of her, and she's going to stay all night, and I was to tell you.'

'All right,' said the giant, majestically.

'All right, all right, all right,' echoed the three little dwarfs.

Then the two woman dwarfs seized Rosalie by the hand and wanted her to sit down and have supper with them. But Rosalie steadily declined; she must not leave her mother nor Mother Manikin.

'Quite right,' said the giant, in a superior voice; 'quite right, child.'

'Quite right, child, quite right,' repeated the three little dwarfs.

Then they escorted Rosalie to the door of the show and bowed her gracefully out.

'Tell Mother Manikin not to come home in daylight,' called the giant, as Rosalie was disappearing through the canvas.

'No, no,' said the three dwarfs; 'not in daylight!'

'Why not?' said Rosalie.

'Our pennies,' said the giant, mysteriously.

F

'Yes, our pennies and halfpennies for seeing the show,' repeated the dwarfs; 'we must not make ourselves too cheap.'

'Good-night, child,' said the giant.

'Good-night, child,' said the dwarfs.

Sorrowful as she was, they almost made Rosalie smile, they were such tiny little creatures to call her 'child' in that superior manner. But she hastened back to the caravan, and, after telling Mother Manikin that she had delivered her message to her friends, she took up her place by her mother's side.

It was a great comfort having little Mother Manikin there, she was so kind and considerate, so thoughtful and clever, and she always seemed to know exactly what was wanted; though Rosalie's mother was too weak to ask for anything.

All night long the poor woman lay still, sometimes entirely unconscious, at other times opening her eyes and trying to smile at poor little Rosalie, who was sitting at the foot of the bed. Mother Manikin did everything that had to be done. She was evidently accustomed to a sick-room, and knew the best way of making those she nursed comfortable. She climbed on a chair and arranged the pillows, so that the sick woman could breathe most easily.

After a time she made the poor tired child take off her white dress, and lie down at the foot of the bed, wrapped in a woollen shawl. And in a few minutes Rosalie fell asleep.

When she awoke, the grey light was stealing in at the caravan window. She raised herself on the bed and looked round. At first she thought she was dreaming, but presently the recollection of the

night before came back to her. There was her
mother sleeping quietly on the bed, and there was
little Mother Manikin sitting faithfully at her post,
never having allowed herself to sleep all that long
night, lest the sick woman should wake and want
something which she could not get.

'Oh, Mother Manikin,' said Rosalie, getting
down from the bed and throwing her arms round
the little old woman's neck, 'how good you
are!'

'Hush, child!' said the dwarf; 'don't wake your
mother; she's sleeping so peacefully now, and has
been for the last hour.'

'I'm so glad!' said Rosalie; 'do you think she
will soon be better, Mother Manikin?'

'I can't say, my dear; we'll leave that just now.
Tell me what that picture is about up there? I've
been looking at it all night.'

'Oh, that's my picture,' said Rosalie; 'that
shepherd has been looking for that lamb everywhere, and at last he has found it, and is carrying
it home on his shoulder; and he is so glad it is
found though he has hurt himself very much in
looking for it.'

'What is that reading underneath?' said the
little old woman. 'I can't read, my dear, you see;
I am no scholar.'

'"Rejoice with me; for I have found my sheep
which was lost. There is joy in the presence of the
angels of God over one sinner that repenteth".'

'What does that mean, child?' said the old
woman.

'It means Jesus is like the shepherd, and He is

looking for us, Mother Manikin; and it makes Him so glad when He finds us.'

The dwarf nodded her head in assent.

'We ask Him every day to find us, Mother Manikin—mummy and me; and the story says He will look for us until He finds us. Shall I read it to you? It's what mummy and I were reading before we went into the play.'

Rosalie went to the box and brought out the little Testament, and then, sitting at Mother Manikin's feet, she read her favourite story of the lost sheep.

'Has He found you, Mother Manikin?' she said, as she closed the book.

The little dwarf put her head on one side, and smoothed her tiny grey curls, but made no answer. Rosalie was almost afraid she had vexed her, and did not like to say anything more. But a long time afterwards—so long that Rosalie had been thinking of a dozen things since—Mother Manikin answered her question, and said in a strange whisper:

'No, child; He *hasn't* found *me*.'

'Won't you ask Him, dear Mother Manikin?' said Rosalie.

'Yes, child; I'll begin to-day,' said the little dwarf. 'I'll begin now, if you'll say the words for me.'

Rosalie slipped down from her stool, and, kneeling on the floor of the caravan she said, aloud:

'O Good Shepherd, you are looking for mummy and me; please look for Mother Manikin too; and please put her on your shoulder and carry her home. Amen.'

'Amen!' said old Mother Manikin in her hoarse whisper.

She did not talk any more after this. About six o'clock there came a rap on the caravan door, and a woman in a long cloak appeared, asking if Mother Manikin were there. She belonged to the Royal Show of Dwarfs, and she had come to take Mother Manikin home before the business of the market-place commenced. Some men were already passing by to their work; so the woman wrapped Mother Manikin in a shawl, and carried her home like a baby, covering her with her cloak, so that no one should see who she was. Rosalie thanked her with tears in her eyes for all her kindness; and the little woman promised soon to come again and see how her patient was.

CHAPTER 9

THE DOCTOR'S VISIT

ROSALIE was not long alone after Mother Manikin
left her. There was a rap at the door, and on
opening it she found Toby.

'Miss Rosie,' he said, 'how is she now?'

'I think she is sleeping quietly, Toby,' said Rosalie.

'I would have come before, but I was afraid of
disturbing her,' said Toby. 'I've been thinking of
her all night; I didn't get many winks of sleep,
Miss Rosie!'

'Oh! Toby, was it you that fetched little Mother
Manikin?'

'Yes, Miss Rosie; I used to belong to their show
before I came to master; and once I had a fever,
and Mother Manikin nursed me all the time I had
it, so I knew she would know what to do.'

'She *is* a kind little thing,' said Rosalie.

'Yes, missie; she has only got a little body, but
there's a great kind heart inside it. But, Miss
Rosie, I wanted to tell you something; I'm going
to fetch a doctor to see missis.'

'Oh, Toby! but what will my father say?'

'It's he that has sent me, Miss Rosie; you see,
I think he's ashamed. You should have seen the
men last night, when they were shutting up the
theatre after you had gone away. They went up
to master, and gave him a bit of their minds about
letting missis come on the stage when she was so

ill. They told him it was a sin and a shame the way he treated her, taking less care of her than if she were one of his old horses (not that he's over and above good to them neither). Well, master didn't like it, Miss Rosie, and he was very angry at the time; but this morning, as soon as it was light, he told me to get up at seven o'clock and fetch a doctor to see missis at once. So I thought I'd better tell you, Miss Rosie, that you might put things straight before he comes.'

As soon as Toby had gone, Rosalie put the caravan in order and awaited anxiously the doctor's arrival. Her father brought him in, and stayed in the caravan while he felt the poor woman's pulse, and asked Rosalie several questions about her cough, which from time to time was so distressing. Then they went out together, and little Rosalie was left in suspense. She had not dared to ask the doctor what he thought of her mother when her father was present, and her little heart was full of anxious fear.

Augustus came in soon after the doctor had left; and Rosalie crept up to him, and asked what he had said of her mother.

'He says she is very ill,' said her father, shortly and in a voice which told Rosalie that she must ask no more questions. And then he sat down beside the bed for about half an hour, and looked more softened than Rosalie had ever seen him before. She was sure the doctor must have told him that her mother was very bad indeed.

Rosalie's father did not speak; there was no sound in the caravan but the ticking of the little clock which was fastened to a nail in the corner, and the occasional falling of the cinders in the ash-pan. Augustus' reflections were not pleasant as he sat by his wife's dying bed. For the doctor had told him she would never be better, and it was only a question of time how long she would live. And when Augustus heard that, all his cruel treatment came back to his mind—the hard words he had spoken to her, the unkind things he had said of her, and above all, the hard-hearted way in which he had made her come on the stage the night before, when she was almost too ill to stand. All these things crowded in on his memory, and a short fit of remorse seized him. It was this which led him, contrary to his custom, to come into the caravan and sit by her side.

But his meditations became so unpleasant at length, that he could bear them no longer; he could not sit there and face the accusations of his conscience; so he jumped up hastily, and went out without saying a word to his child, slammed the little caravan door after him, and sauntered down the market-place. Here he met some of his friends, who rallied him on his melancholy appearance, and offered to treat him to a glass in the nearest public-house. And there Augustus Joyce banished all thoughts of his wife, and stifled the loud accusing voice of his conscience. When he returned to the theatre for dinner, he appeared as hard and selfish as ever, and never even asked how his wife was before he sat down to eat. Perhaps he dreaded to hear the answer to that question.

That evening Rosalie was obliged to take her part in the play; her father insisted on it; it was impossible for him to spare her, he said, and to fill up both her place and her mother's also. Rosalie begged him most earnestly to excuse her, but all in vain; so with an aching heart she went to the Royal Show of Dwarfs and asked for Mother Manikin.

The good little woman was indignant when Rosalie told her she was not allowed to stay with her mother, and promised immediately to come and sit beside the poor woman in her absence. The other dwarfs rather grumbled at this arrangement; but Mother Manikin shook her little fist at them, and called them hard-hearted creatures, and declared that old age must have its liberties. She had been entertaining the company all the afternoon, and must have a little rest this evening.

'Oh! Mother Manikin,' said Rosalie, 'and you had no sleep last night.'

'Oh! my dear, I'm all right,' said the good little woman. 'I had a nap or two this morning. Don't trouble about me; and Miss Mab and Master Puck ought to be ashamed of themselves for wanting me when there's that poor dear thing so ill out there. Bless me, my dears!' said the old woman, turning to the dwarfs, 'what should you want with an ugly little thing like me? It's you lovely young creatures that the company comes to see. So I'll wish you good-night, my dears. Take care of yourselves, and don't get into any mischief when I'm away! Where's Susannah!'

'Here, ma'am,' said the woman who had come for Mother Manikin that morning.

'Carry me to Joyce's van,' said the little old

woman, jumping on a chair and holding out her arms.

Susannah wrapped her in her cloak, and took her quickly in the direction of the theatre, Rosalie walking by her side.

Then the little woman helped the child to dress —pulling out the folds of her white dress for her, and combing her long hair in a most motherly fashion. When the child was ready, she stood looking sorrowfully at her mother's pale face. But as she was looking her mother's eyes opened, and gazed lovingly and tenderly at her, and then, to the child's joy, her mother spoke.

'Rosalie, darling!' she whispered, 'I feel better to-night. Kiss your mother, Rosie.'

The child bent down and kissed her mother's face, and her long dark hair lay across her mother's pillow.

'Who is it taking care of me, Rosalie?'

'It's a little woman Toby knows, mummy dear; she's so kind, and she says she will sit with you all the time I'm out. I didn't want to leave you —oh! I wanted so much to stay, but I could not be spared, father says.'

'Never mind, darling,' said her mother. 'I feel a little better to-night. I should like a cup of tea.'

Mother Manikin had a cup of tea ready almost directly. She was the quickest little body Rosalie had ever seen; yet she was so quiet that her quick movements did not in the least disturb the sick woman.

'How kind you are!' said Rosalie's mother, as the dwarf climbed on a chair to give her the tea.

'There's nothing like tea,' said the tiny old woman, nodding her wise little head; 'give me a cup of tea, and I don't care what I go without! You're better to-night, ma'am.'

'Yes,' said Rosalie's mother; 'I can talk a little now. I heard a great deal you said before, though I could not speak to you. I heard you talking about Rosalie's picture.'

'To think of that!' said the little old woman, cheerily. 'To think of that, Rosalie! Why, she heard us talking; bless me, child, she's not so bad after all.'

'I think that did me good,' said the poor woman; 'I heard Rosalie pray.'

'Yes,' said Mother Manikin; 'she put me in her prayer, bless her! I haven't forgotten that!'

Then Rosalie's mother seemed very tired, and her careful nurse would not let her talk any more, but made her lie quite quietly without moving. When Rosalie left her to go on the stage she was sleeping peacefully, with kind Mother Manikin sitting by her side. And when the child returned late at night there she was sitting still. And she insisted on Rosalie's undressing and creeping into bed beside her mother, that she might have a proper night's rest. For poor little Rosalie was completely exhausted with the stifling air, the fatigue, and the anxiety to which she had been subjected.

The next day her mother seemed to have revived a little and was able to take a little food, and to talk to her in whispers from time to time.

'Rosalie,' she said that afternoon, 'there is a verse come back to me which our nurse taught me;

I haven't thought of it for years, but that night when I was so ill I woke saying it.'

'What is it, mummy dear?' said Rosalie.

'"All we like sheep have gone astray; we have turned every one to his own way: and the Lord hath laid on Him the iniquity of us all." That was it, dear.'

'Mother Manikin told me you said something about sheep, mummy.'

'Yes, that was it,' said the poor woman; 'it's such a beautiful verse! "All we like sheep have gone astray," that's just like me, darling. I've gone astray, oh! so far astray. "And have turned every one to his own way." That's me again—my own way, that's just what it was;—I chose it myself; I would have my own way. It's just like me, Rosalie.'

'And what's the end of the verse, mummy dear?'

'"The Lord hath laid on Him the iniquity of us all." That means Jesus; the Lord put all our sins on Him when He died on the cross.'

'Did God put your sins on Jesus, mummy dear?'

'Yes, child; I think it must mean mine, because it says "the iniquity of us *all*." I think "all" must take me in, Rosalie; at least I hope so. I have been asking Him to let it take me in, because, you know, if the sin is laid on Him, Rosie darling, I shan't have to bear it too.'

The poor woman was quite exhausted when she had said this; and Rosalie brought her some beef-tea which Mother Manikin had made for her, and which was simmering on the stove. The good little woman came once more to stay with Rosalie's mother while the play was going on.

The theatre closed rather earlier that night, for a large fair was to be held at a town some way off, at which Augustus Joyce was very anxious to be present; and as he did not think there was much more to be done in Lesborough, he determined to start at once. So, the moment that the last person had left the theatre, Augustus and his men hastily put off the clothes in which they had been acting, slipped on their working coats, and began to pull down the scenery.

All night long they were hammering and knocking down and packing up, and when morning dawned they were ready to start.

They were not the only ones who had been packing up all night. There were several other fairs drawing near, at which the show-people had taken ground; so they worked away as those who had no time to lose.

'Miss Rosie,' said Toby's voice at about five o'clock that morning, 'they are all going off except us. Master says we can wait a bit longer, to give missis a little more rest. He and the other men are going off at once, to get the theatre set up and everything ready, and master says it will be time enough if we are there by the first night of the fair. He can't do without you then, he says.'

'I am very glad mummy hasn't to be moved just yet,' said Rosalie; 'the shaking would hurt her so much, I'm sure.'

Augustus came into the caravan for a few minutes before he set off. He told Rosalie that they might stay two days longer; but on Saturday morning they must be off early, so as to get into the town on Sunday night.

'I wouldn't have you away from the play in this town, Rosalie, not for the world. It's a large seaside place, and I hope to make a pretty penny there, if every one does their duty.'

'Augustus,' said his wife in a trembling voice, 'can you stay five minutes with me before you go?'

'Well,' said Augustus, taking out his watch, 'perhaps I might spare five minutes; but you must be quick. I ought to be off by now.'

'Rosalie darling,' said her mother, 'leave me and your father alone.'

Little Rosalie went down the steps of the caravan, shutting the door gently behind her, and stood watching her father's men, who were putting the horses in the shafts and tying ropes round the different loads, to prevent anything falling off.

As soon as she was gone, her mother laid her hand on her husband's arm, and said:

'Augustus, there are two things I want to ask you before I die.'

'What are they?' said the man, shortly, crossing his legs and leaning back on his chair.

'The first is, Augustus, that you will find a home for Rosalie when I'm dead. Don't take her about from fair to fair; she will have no mother to take care of her; and I can't bear to think of her being left here all alone.'

'All alone!' said Augustus angrily; 'she will have me; she will be all right if I'm here; and I'm not going to let the child go just when she's beginning to be useful. Besides, where would you have her go?'

Rosalie's mother did not tell the secret hope

which was in her heart. 'I thought,' she said, 'you might find some motherly body in the country somewhere, who would take care of her for very little money, and would send her to school regularly, and see she was brought up properly.'

'Oh, nonsense!' said Augustus; 'she will be all right with me; and I'm not going to lose a pretty child like·that from the stage! Why, half the people come to see the lovely little actress, as they call her; I know better than to spoil her for acting by putting her down in some slow country place. Well, the five minutes are up,' said Augustus, looking at his watch; 'I must be off.'

'There was something else I wanted to ask you, Augustus.'

'Well, what is it? Be quick!'

'I wanted to tell you that the last fortnight I have been feeling that when one comes to die, there is nothing in this world worth having, except to know that your soul is safe. I've led a wicked life, Augustus; I've often been disagreeable and bad to you; but all my desire now is that the Good Shepherd should seek me and find me, before it is too late.'

'Is that all?' said her husband, putting on his coat.

'No, Augustus; I wanted to ask you something. Are *you* ready to die?'

'There's time enough to think of that,' said her husband, with a laugh.

Yet there was an uneasy expression in his face as he said it, which showed that the answer to the question was not a satisfactory one.

'Oh, Augustus! you don't know how long t____ may be,' said his poor wife, sorrowfully.

'Well,' said he, 'if life's so short, we must get all the play we can out of it!'

'But what of the other life, Augustus—the long life that's coming?'

'Oh! that may take care of itself,' said her husband, scornfully, as he lighted his pipe at the stove; and, wishing his wife a pleasant journey, he went down the steps of the caravan and closed the door.

The poor wife turned over on her pillow and wept. She had made a very great effort in speaking to her husband, and it had been of no avail. She was so spent and exhausted that, had it not been for Mother Manikin's beef-tea, which Rosalie gave her as soon as she came in, she must have fainted from very weariness.

A few minutes afterwards some of the wagons rumbled past, the theatre party set off on their journey, and Rosalie and her mother were left alone.

CHAPTER 10

BRITANNIA

ALL day long the packing up went on, and one by
one the shows moved off, and the market-place
became more empty.

In the afternoon Toby came to the caravan to
inform Rosalie that the 'Royal Show of Dwarfs'
was just going to start, and Mother Manikin wanted
to say good-bye to her.

'Mind you thank her, Rosalie,' said the sick
woman, 'and give her my love.'

'Yes, mummy dear,' said the child. 'I won't
forget.'

She found the four little dwarfs sitting in a tiny
covered wagon, in which they were to take their
journey. Rosalie was cautiously admitted, and the
door closed carefully after her. Mother Manikin
took leave of her with tears in her eyes; they were
not going to the same fair as Rosalie's father, and
she did not know when they would meet again.
She gave Rosalie very particular directions about
the beef-tea, and slipped in her pocket a tiny
parcel which she told her to give to her mother.
And then she whispered in Rosalie's ear:

'I haven't forgotten to ask the Good Shepherd
to find me, child; and don't you leave me out, my
dear, when you say your prayers at night.'

'Come, Mother Manikin,' said Master Puck, 'we
must be off!'

Mother Manikin shook her fist at him, saying:

'Old age must have its liberties,' and 'young things should not be so impatient.'

Then she put her little arms round Rosalie's neck and kissed and hugged her; and the three other dwarfs insisted on kissing her too. And as soon as Rosalie had gone the signal was given for their departure, and the 'Royal Show of Dwarfs' left the market-place.

Rosalie ran home to her mother and gave her Mother Manikin's parcel. There were several paper wrappings, which the child took off one by one, and then came an envelope, inside which was a piece of money. She took it out and held it up to her mother; it was a half-sovereign!

Good little Mother Manikin! she had taken the half-sovereign from her small bag of savings, and she had put it in that envelope with even a gladder heart than Rosalie's mother had when she received it!

'Oh, Rosalie,' said the sick woman, 'I can have some more beef-tea now!'

'Yes,' said the child; 'I'll get the meat at once.'

It was not only at her evening prayer that Rosalie mentioned Mother Manikin's name that day; it was not only then that she knelt down to ask the Good Shepherd to seek and to save little Mother Manikin.

All day long Rosalie sat by her mother's side watching her tenderly and carefully, and trying to imitate Mother Manikin in the way she arranged her pillows and waited on her. And when evening came the large square was quite deserted, except by the scavengers, who were going from one

end to another sweeping up the rubbish which had
been left behind.

Rosalie felt very lonely next day. Toby had slept
at an inn in the town, and was out all day at a
village some miles off, to which his master had
sent him to procure something he wanted at a sale
there. The market-place was quite empty, and no
one came near the one solitary caravan—no one
except an officer of the Ministry of Health, to
inquire what was the cause of the delay, and
whether the sick woman was suffering from any
infectious complaint. People passed down the
market-place and went to the various shops, but
no one came near Rosalie and her mother.

The sick woman slept the greater part of the day,
and spoke very little; but every now and then the
child heard her repeat to herself the last verse of
her little hymn:

> 'Lord, I come without delaying;
>   To Thine arms at once I flee.
> Lest no more I hear Thee saying,
>   "Come, come to Me."'

Then night came, and Rosalie sat by her mother's
side; for she did not like to go to sleep, lest she
should awake and want something. And oh! what
a long night it seemed. The Town-hall clock struck
the quarters, but that was the only sound that
broke the stillness. Rosalie kept a light burning,
and every now and then mended the little fire,
that the beef-tea might be ready whenever her
mother wanted it. And many times she gazed at
her picture, and wished she were the little lamb

safe in the Good Shepherd's arms. For she felt
weary and tired, and longed for rest.

The next morning the child heard Toby's voice
as soon as it was light.

'Miss Rosie,' he said, 'can I come in for a minute?'

Rosalie opened the door, and Toby was much
distressed to see how ill and tired she looked.

'You mustn't make yourself ill, Miss Rosie, you
really mustn't!' he said reproachfully.

'I'll try not, Toby,' said the child; 'perhaps the
country air will do me good.'

'Yes, missie, maybe it will. I think we'd better
start at once, because I don't want to go fast; the
slower we go the better it will be for missis; and
then we will stop somewhere for the night; if we
come to a village we can stop there, and I'll get a
hole in some barn to creep into, or if there's no
village convenient there's sure to be a haystack.
I've slept on a haystack before this, Miss Rosie.'

In about half-an-hour Toby had made all ready,
and they left the market-place. Very slowly and
carefully he drove; yet the shaking tried Rosalie's
mother much. Her cough was exceedingly trouble-
some, and her breathing was very bad. She was
obliged to be propped up with pillows, and even
then she could hardly breathe. The child opened
the caravan door, and every now and then spoke to
Toby, who was sitting just underneath it. He did
not whistle to-day, nor call out to his horse, but
seemed very thoughtful and quiet.

Towards evening Rosalie's mother fell asleep—
such a sweet peaceful sleep it was, that the child
could but wish it to continue. It made her so glad

to hear the coughing cease and the breathing become more regular, and she dreaded lest any jolting of the caravan should awaken her.

'What do you think of stopping here for the night, Miss Rosie?' said Toby.

They had come to a very quiet and solitary place on the borders of a large moor. A great pine-forest stretched on one side of them, and the trees looked dark and solemn in the fading light. At the edge of this wood was a stone wall, against which Toby drew up the caravan, that it might be sheltered from the wind.

On the other side of the road was the moor, stretching on for miles and miles. And on this moor, in a little sheltered corner surrounded by furze-bushes, Toby had determined to sleep.

'I shall be close by, Miss Rosie,' he said. 'I sleep pretty sound; but if only you call out "Toby" I shall be at your side in a twinkling; I always wake in a trice when I hear my name called. You won't be frightened, Miss Rosie, will you?'

'No,' said Rosalie; 'I think not.'

She gazed rather fearfully down the road at the corner of which they had drawn up. The trees were throwing dark shadows across the path, and their branches were waving gloomily in the evening breeze. Rosalie shivered a little as she looked at them and at the dark pine forest behind her.

'I'll tell you what, Miss Rosie,' said Toby, as he finished eating his supper, 'I'll sit on the steps of the caravan if you are frightened at all. No, no; never you mind me; I shall be all right. One night's sitting up won't hurt me!'

Rosalie would not allow it; she insisted on Toby's going to sleep on the heather, and made him take her mother's warm shawl, that he might wrap himself in it, for it was a very cold night. Then she carefully bolted the caravan door, closed the windows, and crept to her sleeping mother's side. She sat on the bed, put her head on the pillow, and tried to sleep also. But the intense stillness was oppressive, and made her head ache, for she kept sitting up in the bed to listen, and to strain her ears—longing for any sounds to break the silence.

Yet when a sound *did* come—when the wind swept over the fir-trees, and made the branches which hung over the caravan creak and sway to and fro—Rosalie trembled with fear. Poor child! the want of sleep the last few nights was telling on her, and had made her nervous and sensitive. At last she found the matches and lighted a candle, that she might not feel quite so lonely.

Then she took her Testament from the box and began to read. As she read, little Rosalie felt no longer alone. She had a strange realization of the Good Shepherd's presence, and a wonderful feeling that her prayer was heard, and that He was indeed carrying her in His bosom.

If it had not been for this, she would have screamed with horror when, about an hour afterwards, there came a tap at the caravan door. Rosalie jumped from her seat, and peeped out between the muslin curtains. She could just see a dark figure crouching on the caravan steps.

'Is it you, Toby?' she said, opening the window cautiously.

'No, it's me,' said a girl's voice; 'have you got a fire in there?'

'Who are you?' said Rosalie fearfully.

'I'll tell you when I get in,' said the girl; 'let me come and warm myself by your fire!'

Rosalie did not know what to do. She did not much like opening the door, for how could she tell who this stranger might be? She had almost determined to call Toby, when the sound of sobbing made her change her mind.

'What's the matter?' she said, addressing the girl.

'I'm cold and hungry and miserable!' she said, with a sob; 'and I saw your light, and I thought you would let me in.'

Rosalie hesitated no longer. She unbolted the door, and the dark figure on the steps came in. She threw off a long cloak with which she was covered; and Rosalie could see that she was quite a young girl, about seventeen years old, and that she had been crying until her eyes were swollen and red. She was as cold as ice; there seemed to be no feeling in her hands, and her teeth chattered as she sat down on the bench by the side of the stove.

Rosalie put some cold tea into a little pan and made it hot. And when the girl had drunk this she seemed better, and more inclined to talk.

'Is that your mother?' she said, glancing at the bed where Rosalie's mother was still sleeping peacefully.

'Yes,' said Rosalie in a whisper, 'we mustn't wake her, she is very, very ill. That's why we didn't start with the rest of the company; and the doctor has given her some medicine to make her sleep while we're travelling.'

'I have a mother,' said the girl.

'Have you?' said Rosalie; 'where is she?'

The girl did not answer this question; she buried her face in her hands and began to cry again.

Rosalie looked at her very sorrowfully; 'I wish you would tell me what's the matter,' she said, 'and who you are.'

'I'm Britannia!' said the girl, without looking up.

'Britannia!' repeated Rosalie, in a puzzled voice; 'what do you mean?'

'You were at Lesborough, weren't you?' said the girl.

'Yes; we've just come from Lesborough.'

'Then didn't you see the circus there?'

'Oh yes,' said Rosalie; 'the procession passed us on the road as we were going into the town.'

'Well, I'm Britannia,' said the girl; 'didn't you see me on the top of the last car? I had a white dress on and a scarlet scarf.'

'Yes,' said Rosalie; 'I remember, and a great fork in your hand.'

'Yes; they called it a trident, and they called me Britannia.'

'But what are you doing here?' asked the child.

'I've run away; I couldn't stand it any longer. I'm going home.'

'Where is your home?' said Rosalie.

'Oh, a long way off,' she said. 'I don't suppose I shall ever get there. I haven't a penny in my pocket, and I'm tired out already. I've been walking all night and all day.'

Then she began to cry again, and sobbed so loudly that Rosalie was afraid she would awaken and alarm her mother.

'Oh, Britannia!' she said; 'don't cry! tell me what's the matter?'

'Call me by my own name,' said the girl, with another sob. 'I'm not Britannia now, I'm Jessie; "Little Jess," my mother always calls me.'

At the mention of her mother she cried again as if her heart would break.

'Jessie,' said Rosalie, laying her hand on her arm, 'won't you tell me about it?'

The girl stopped crying, and as soon as she was calmer she told Rosalie her story.

'I've got such a good mother; it's that which made me cry,' she said.

'Your mother isn't in the circus, then, is she?' said Rosalie.

'Oh no,' said the girl; and she almost smiled through her tears—such a sad, sorrowful attempt at a smile it was: 'you don't know my mother, or you wouldn't ask that! No; she lives in a village a long way from here. I'm going to her; at least I *think* I am; I don't know if I dare.'

'Why not?' said Rosalie; 'are you frightened of your mother?'

'No; I'm not frightened of her,' said the girl; 'but I've been so bad to her, I'm almost ashamed to go back. She doesn't know where I am now. I expect she has had no sleep since I ran away.'

'When did you run away?' asked the child.

'It will be three weeks ago now,' said Jessie, mournfully; 'but it seems more like three months. I never was so wretched in all my life before; I've cried myself to sleep every night.'

'What ever made you leave your mother?' said Rosalie.

'It was that circus; it came to the next town to where we lived. All the girls in the village were going to it, and I wanted to go with them, and my mother wouldn't let me.'

'Why not?'

'She said I should get no good there—that there were a great many bad people went to such places, and I was better away.'

'Then how did you see it?' said Rosalie.

'I didn't see it that day; and at night the girls came home and told me all about it, and what a fine procession it was, and how the women were all dressed in silver and gold, and the men in shining armour. And then I almost cried with disappointment because I had not seen it too. The girls said it would be in the town one more day, and then it was going away. And when I got into bed that night I made up my mind that I would go and have a look at it the next day.'

'Did your mother let you?' said Rosalie.

'No; I knew it was no use asking her. I meant to slip out of the house before she knew anything about it; but it so happened that that day she was called away to the next village to see my aunt, who was ill.'

'Did you go when she was out?'

'Yes, I did,' said Jessie; 'and I told her a lie about it.'

This was said with a great sob, and the poor girl's tears began to flow again.

'What did you say?' asked little Rosalie.

'She said to me before she went, "Little Jess, you'll take care of Maggie and baby, won't you, dear? You'll not let any harm come to them?" and I said, "No, mother, I won't." But as I said it my cheeks turned hot, and I felt as if my mother must see how they were burning. But she did not seem to notice it; she turned back and kissed me, and kissed little Maggie and the baby, and then she went to my aunt's. I watched her out of sight, and then I put on my best clothes and set off for the town.'

'What did you do with Maggie and baby?' said Rosalie; 'did you take them with you?'

'No; that's the worst of it,' said the girl; 'I left them; I put the baby in its crib upstairs, and I told Maggie to look after it, and then I put the table in front of the fire, and locked them in, and put the key in the window. I thought I should only be away a short time.'

'How long were you?'

'When I got to the town the procession was just passing, and I stopped to look at it. And when I saw the men and women sitting up on the cars, I thought they were kings and queens. Well, I went to the circus and saw all that there was to be seen; and then I looked at the church clock, and found it was five o'clock, for the exhibition had not been till the afternoon. I knew my mother would be home, and I did not like to go back; I wondered what she would say to me about leaving the children. So I walked round the circus for some time looking at the gilded cars which were drawn up in the field. And as I was looking at them an old man came up to me and began talking to me. He asked me what I thought of the circus; and I told him I thought it splendid. Then he asked me what I liked best, and I said these women in gold and silver who were sitting on the gilt cars.

'"Would you like to be dressed like that?" he said.

'"Yes, that I should," I said, as I looked down at my dress—my best dress which I had once thought so smart.

'"Well," he said, mysteriously, "I don't know, but perhaps I may get you that chance; just wait here a minute, and I'll see."

'I stood there trembling, hardly knowing what to wish. At last he came back, and told me to follow him. He took me into a room, and there I found a very grand woman—at least she looked like one then. She asked me if I would like to come and be Britannia in the circus and ride on the gilt car.'

'What did you say?' asked Rosalie.

'I thought it was a great chance for me, and I told her I would stay. I was so excited about it that I hardly knew where I was; it seemed just as if someone was asking me to be a queen. And it was not till I got into bed that I let myself think of my mother.'

'Did you think of her then?' said Rosalie.

'Yes, I couldn't help thinking of her then; but

there were six or seven other girls in the room, and I was afraid of them hearing me cry, so I hid my face under the bed-clothes. The next day we moved from that town; and I felt very miserable all the time we were travelling. Then the circus was set up again, and we went in the procession.'

'Did you like that?' asked the child.

'No; it was not as nice as I expected. It was a cold day, and the white dress was very thin, and oh! I was so dizzy on that car; I was very high up and I felt every moment as if I should fall. And then they were so unkind to me. I was very miserable because I kept thinking of my mother; and when they were talking and laughing I used to cry, and they didn't like that. They said I was very different from the last girl they had. She had left them to be married, and they were looking out for a fresh girl when they met me. They thought I had a pretty face, and would do very well. But they were angry with me for looking so miserable, and found more and more fault with me.

'They were always quarrelling; long after we went to bed they were shouting at each other. Oh! I got so tired of it; I *did* wish I had never left home. And then we came to Lesborough, and at last I could bear it no longer. I kept dreaming about my mother, and when I woke in the night I thought I heard my mother's voice. At last I determined to run away. I knew they would be very angry; but no money could make me put up with that sort of life; I was thoroughly sick of it. I felt ill and weary, and longed for my mother. And now I'm going home. I ran away the night they left Lesborough. I got out of the caravan when they were all asleep. I've been walking ever since; I brought a little food with me; but it's all gone now, and how I shall get home I don't know.'

'Poor Jessie!' said little Rosalie.

'I don't know what my mother will say when I get there. I know she won't scold me; I shouldn't mind that half so much, but I can't bear to see my mother cry.'

'She *will* be glad to get you back,' said Rosalie. 'I don't know what my mummy would do if I ran away.'

'Oh dear!' said Jessie, 'I hope nothing came to those children; I do hope they got no harm when I was out; I've thought about that so often.'

Then the poor girl seemed very tired, and leaning against the wall she fell asleep, while Rosalie rested once more against her mother's pillow. And again there was no sound to be heard but the wind sweeping among the dark fir-trees. Rosalie was glad to have Jessie there; it did not seem quite so solitary.

At last rest was given to the tired little woman; her eyes closed, and she forgot her troubles in a sweet, refreshing sleep.

THE MOTHER'S DREAM

WHEN Rosalie awoke, her mother's eyes were fixed on her, and she was sitting up in bed. Her breathing was very painful, and she was holding her hand to her side, as if she were in much pain.

The candle had burnt low in the socket, and the early morning light was stealing into the caravan. Jessie was still asleep in the corner, with her head leaning against the wall.

'Rosalie,' said her mother, under her breath, 'where are we, and who is that girl?'

'We're half way to the town, mummy—out on a moor; and that's Britannia!'

'What do you mean?' asked her mother.

'It's the girl we saw riding on that gilt car in Lesborough, and she has run away, she was so miserable there.'

Then Rosalie told her mother the sad story she had just heard.

'Poor thing! poor young thing!' said the sick woman. 'I'm glad you took her in; mind you give her a good breakfast. She does well to go back to her mother; it's the best thing she can do. Is she asleep, Rosalie?'

'Yes, mummy dear, she went to sleep before I did.'

'Do you think it would wake her if you were to sing to me?'

'No, mummy dear, I shouldn't think so, if I didn't sing very loud.'

'Then could you sing me your hymn once more? I've had the tune in my ears all night, and I should so much like to hear it.'

So little Rosalie sang her hymn. She had a sweet low voice, and she sang very correctly; if she had heard a tune once she never forgot it.

When she had finished singing Jessie moved, and opened her eyes, and looked up with a smile, as if she were in the midst of a pleasant dream. Then, as she saw the inside of the caravan, the sick woman, and Rosalie, she remembered where she was, and burst into tears.

'What's the matter?' said the child, running up to her, and putting her arms round her neck; 'were you thinking of your mother?'

'No, dear,' she said; 'I was dreaming.'

'Ask her what she was dreaming,' said Rosalie's mother.

'I was dreaming I was at home, and it was Sunday, and we were at the Bible-class, and singing the hymn we always begin with. I was singing it when I woke, and it made me cry to think it wasn't true.'

'Perhaps it was my singing that made you dream it,' said Rosalie; 'I've been singing to my mummy.'

'Oh! I should think that was it,' said the girl. 'What did you sing? Will you sing it to me?'

Rosalie sang over again the first verse of the hymn. To her surprise Jessie started from her seat and seized her by the hand.

'Where did you get that?' she asked hurriedly; 'that's the very hymn I was singing in my dream. We always sing it on Sunday afternoons at our Bible-class.'

'I have it on a card,' said Rosalie, bringing her favourite card down from the wall.

'Why, who gave you that?' said the girl; 'it's just like mine; mine has a ribbon in it just that colour. Where *did* you get it?'

'We were passing through a village,' said Rosalie, 'and a kind woman gave it to me. We stopped there about an hour, and she was singing it outside her cottage door.'

'Why, it must have been our village, surely!' said Jessie; 'I don't think they have those cards anywhere else! What was the woman like?'

'She was a young woman with a very nice face; she had one little boy about two years old, and he was playing with his ball in front of the house. His mother was so good to us—she gave us some bread and milk.'

'Why, it must have been Mrs. Barker!' said the girl; 'she lives close to us; our cottage is just a little farther up the road; she often sings when she's at work. To think that you've been to our village! Oh! I wish you'd seen my mother!'

'Do you know Mrs. Leslie?' asked the sick woman, raising herself in bed.

'Yes, that I do,' said the girl. 'She's our clergyman's wife—such a kind woman—oh, she *is* good to us! I'm in her Bible-class; we go to the vicarage every Sunday afternoon. Do *you* know her?' she asked, turning to Rosalie's mother.

H

'I used to know her many years ago,' said the sick woman; 'but it's a long, long time since I saw her.'

Rosalie crept up to her mother's side, and put her little hand in hers; for she knew that the mention of her sister would bring back all the sorrowful memories of the past. But the sick woman was very calm to-day; she did not seem at all ruffled or disturbed, but she lay looking at Jessie with her eyes half-closed. It seemed as if she were pleased even to look at someone who had seen her sister Lucy.

About six o'clock Toby came to the caravan door, and asked how his mistress was, and if they were ready to start. He was very surprised when he saw Jessie sitting inside the caravan. But Rosalie told him in a few words how the poor girl came there and asked him in what direction she ought to walk to get to her own home. Toby was very clever in knowing the way to nearly every place in the country, and he said that for ten miles farther their roads would be the same, and Jessie could ride with them in the caravan.

The poor girl was very grateful to them for all their kindness. She sat beside Rosalie's mother all the morning, and did everything she could for her. The effect of the doctor's medicine had passed off, and the sick woman was very restless and wakeful. She was burnt with fever, and tossed about from side to side of her bed. Every now and then her mind seemed to wander, and she talked of her mother and of her sister Lucy, and of other things which Rosalie did not understand. Then she became quite sensible, and would repeat over and over again the words of the hymn, or would ask Rosalie to read to her once more about the lost sheep and the Good Shepherd.

When the child had read the parable the mother turned to Jessie, and said to her, very earnestly:

'Oh! do ask the Good Shepherd to find you now, Jessie; you'll be so glad of it afterwards!'

'I've been so bad!' said Jessie, crying. 'My mother has often talked to me, and Mrs. Leslie has too; and yet after all I've gone and done this. I daren't ever ask Him to find me now.'

'Why not, Jessie?' said Rosalie's mother; 'why not ask Him?'

'Oh! He would have nothing to say to me now,' said the girl, sobbing, and hiding her face in her hands; 'if I'd only gone to Him that Sunday!'

'What Sunday?' asked Rosalie.

'It was the Sunday before I left home. Mrs. Leslie talked to us about coming to Jesus. She asked us if we had come to Him to have our sins forgiven; and she said, "if you haven't come to Him already, do come to Him to-day." And then she begged those of us who hadn't come to Him before to go home when the class was over, and kneel down in our own rooms and ask Jesus to forgive us that very afternoon. I knew *I* had never come to Jesus, and I made up my mind that I would do as our teacher asked us. But, as soon as we were outside the vicarage, the girls began talking and laughing, and made fun of somebody's hat that they had seen at church that morning. And when I got home I thought no more of coming to Jesus, and I never went to him;—and oh! I wish that I had!'

'Go now,' said Rosalie's mother.

'It wouldn't be any good,' said the girl, sorrowfully; 'if I thought it would—if I only thought He would forgive me, I would do anything—I would walk twice the distance home!'

'"He goeth after that which is lost until He find it,"' said the sick woman. 'Are *you* lost, Jessie?'

'Yes,' said the girl; 'that's just what I am!'

'Then He is going after you,' said Rosalie's mother again.

Jessie walked to the door of the caravan, and sat looking out without speaking. The sunlight was streaming on the purple heather, which was spread like a carpet on both sides of the road. Quiet little roadside springs trickled through the moss and ran across the path. The travellers had left the pine-forest behind, and there was not a single tree in sight—nothing but large grey rocks and occasional patches of bright yellow furze among the miles and miles of heath-covered moor.

At last they came to a large signpost, at a corner where four roads met; and here Toby said Jessie must leave them. But before she went there was a little whispered conversation between Rosalie and her mother, which ended in Jessie's carrying away in her pocket no less than half of Mother Manikin's present.

'You'll need it before you get home, dear,' said the sick woman, 'and mind you go straight to your mother. Don't stop till you run right into her arms! And when you see Mrs. Leslie, just tell her you met with a poor woman in a caravan called Norah, who knew her many years ago.'

'Yes,' said Jessie; 'I'll tell her!'

'And say that I sent my respects—my love to her; and tell her I have not very long to live, but the Good Shepherd has sought me and found me, and I'm not afraid to die. Don't forget to tell her that.'

'No,' said Jessie; 'I'll be sure to remember.'

The poor girl was very sorry to leave them; she kissed Rosalie and her mother many times; and as she went down the road she kept turning round to wave her handkerchief, till the caravan was quite out of sight.

'So those girls knew nothing about it, Rosalie darling,' said her mother, when Jessie was gone.

'Nothing about what, mummy dear?'

'Don't you remember the girls that stood by our caravan when the procession went past? They wished they were Britannia, and thought she must be so happy and glad.'

'Oh yes!' said Rosalie; 'they knew nothing about it. All the time poor Jessie was so miserable she did not know what to do with herself.'

'It's just the mistake I made, Rosalie darling, till I came behind the scenes, and knew how different everything looks when one is there. And so it is, dear, with everything in this world; it is all disappointing and vain when one gets to know it well.'

As evening drew on they left the moor behind, and turned into a very dark and shady road with trees on both sides of the way. Rosalie's mother was sleeping for the first time since early morning,

and Rosalie sat and looked out at the door of the
caravan. The wood was very thick, and the long
shadows of the trees fell across the road. Every now
and then they disturbed four or five rabbits that
were enjoying themselves by the side of the path,
and ran headlong into their snug little holes as soon
as they heard the creaking of the caravan-wheels.
Then an owl startled Rosalie by hooting in a tree
overhead, and then several wood-pigeons cooed
mournfully their sad good-nights.

The road was full of turnings, and wound in and
out among the wood. Toby whistled a tune as he
went along, and Rosalie sat and listened to him,
quite glad that he broke the silence. She was not
sorry when they left the wood behind and came
into the open country. And at last there glimmered
in the distance the lights of a village, where Toby
said they would spend the night. He pulled up the
caravan by the wayside, and begged a bed for himself in a barn belonging to one of the small village
farms.

The next day was Sunday. Such a calm, quiet
day, the very air seemed full of Sabbath rest. The
country children were just going to the Sunday-
school as the caravan started. Their mothers had
carefully dressed them and were watching them
down the village street.

The sick woman had been restless and tired all
night. Little Rosalie had watched beside her, and
was weary and sad. Her poor mother had tossed
from side to side of her bed, and could find no
position in which she was comfortable. Again and
again the child altered her mother's pillow, and

tried to make her more easy; but though the poor woman thanked her very gently, not many minutes had passed before she wanted to be moved again.

The Sunday stillness seemed to have a soothing effect on the sick woman; and as they left the village she fell asleep.

For hours that sleep lasted; and when she awoke she seemed refreshed and rested.

'Rosalie darling,' she said, calling her little girl to her side, 'I've had such a beautiful dream!'

'What was it mummy dear?' asked Rosalie.

'I thought I was looking into heaven, Rosalie dear, in between the bars of the golden gates; and I saw all the people dressed in white walking up and down the streets of the city. And then somebody seemed to call them together, and they all went in one direction, and there was a beautiful sound of singing and joy, as if they had heard some good news. One of them passed close to the gate where I was standing, Rosalie, and he looked so happy and glad, as he was hastening on to join the others. So I called him, darling, and asked him what was going on.'

'And what did he say, mummy dear?'

'He said, "it's the Good Shepherd who has called us; He wants us to rejoice with Him; He has just found one of the lost sheep, which He has been seeking so long. Did not you hear His voice just now, when He called us all together? didn't you hear Him saying: Rejoice with Me! for I have found My sheep which was lost?"

'Then they all began to sing again, and, somehow I knew they were singing for *me*, and that *I* was the sheep that was found. And then I was so glad that I awoke with joy! And oh Rosalie darling! I know my dream was true, for I've been asking Him to find me again and again, and I'm quite sure that He wanted to do it, long before I asked Him.'

'Oh, mummy dear!' said Rosalie, putting her hand in her mother's, 'I *am* so glad!'

Rosalie's mother did not talk any more then; but she lay very quietly, holding Rosalie's hand, and every now and then she smiled, as if the music of the heavenly song were still in her ears, and as if she still heard the Good Shepherd saying, 'Rejoice with Me, for I have found My sheep which was lost.'

Then they passed through another village, where the bells were ringing for afternoon service, and the sick woman listened to them very sorrowfully.

'I shall never go to church again, Rosalie darling,' she said.

'Oh, mummy!' said little Rosalie; 'don't talk like that! When you get better we'll go together. We could easily slip into the back seats where nobody would see us.'

'No, Rosalie,' said her mother; 'you may go, my darling, but *I* never shall.'

'Why not, mummy dear?'

'Rosalie,' said her mother, raising herself in bed and putting her arm round her child, 'don't you know that I'm going to leave you? Don't you know that in about a week's time you will have no mother?'

Rosalie hid her face in her mother's pillow and sobbed aloud.

'Oh, mummy, mummy dear—mummy, don't say that! Please don't say that!'

'It's true, little Rosalie,' said her mother; 'and I want you to know it. I don't want it to take you by surprise. And now stop crying, darling, for I want to talk to you a bit; I want to tell you some things while I can speak.

'My poor, poor darling!' said the mother, as the child continued sobbing.

She stroked her little girl's head very gently; and after a long, long time the sobbing ceased, and Rosalie only cried quietly.

'Little woman,' said her mother, 'can you listen to me now?'

Rosalie pressed her mother's hand, but she could not answer her.

'Rosalie darling, you won't be sorry for your mother; will you, dear? The Good Shepherd has found me, and I'm going to see Him. I'm going to see Him, and thank Him, darling; you mustn't cry for me. And I want to tell you what to do when I'm dead. I've asked your father to let you leave the caravan, and live in some country village; but he won't give his consent, darling; he says he can't spare you. So, dear, you must keep very quiet. Sit in the caravan and read your little Testament by yourself; don't go wandering about the fair, darling. I've been asking the Good Shepherd to take care of you: I told Him you would soon be a little motherless lamb with nobody to look after you, and I asked Him to put you in His bosom and carry you along. And I believe He will, Rosalie dear; I don't think He'll let you get wrong. But you must ask Him yourself, my darling; you must never let a day pass without asking Him: promise your mother, Rosalie—let her hear you say the words.'

'Yes, mummy dear,' said Rosalie, 'I promise you.'

'If ever you can go to your aunt Lucy, you must go to her and give her that letter; you remember where it is; and tell her, dear, that I shall see her some day in that city I dreamed about. I should never have seen her there if it had not been for the Shepherd's love; but He took such pains to find me, and He wouldn't give it up, and at last He put me on His shoulders and carried me home. I am very tired, Rosalie darling, but there is more that I wanted to say. I wanted to tell you that it will not do for you to ask your father about going to your aunt Lucy, because he would never let you, and he would only be writing to her for money if he knew where she lived. But if you go through that village again, you might just run up to the house and give her the letter. I don't know if that would do either,' said the poor woman sadly; 'but God will find you a way. I believe you will get there some day. I can't talk any more now, darling, I *am* so tired! Kiss me, my own little woman.'

Rosalie lifted up a very white and sorrowful face, and kissed her mother passionately.

'You couldn't sing your little hymn, could you, darling?' said the sick woman.

Rosalie tried her very best to sing it, but her voice trembled so that she could not manage it. She struggled through the first verse, but in the

second she quite broke down, and burst into a
fresh flood of tears. Her poor mother tried to soothe
her, but was too weak and weary to do more than
stroke the child's face with her thin, wasted hand,
and whisper in her ear a few words of love.

Very sorrowful were poor Rosalie's thoughts as
she sat by her mother's bed. She had known before
that her mother was very ill; and sometimes she
had been afraid as she thought of the future; but
she had never before heard that dreadful fear put
into words; she had never before known that it
was not merely a fear but a terrible reality. 'In
about a week's time you will have no mother';
that was what her mother had told her.

Her mother was everything to Rosalie. She had
never known a father's love or care; Augustus had
never acted as a father to her. But her mother—
her mother had been everything to her, from the
day she was born until now. Rosalie could not
imagine what the world would be like without her
mother. She could hardly fancy herself living when
her mother was dead. She would have no one to
speak to her, no one to care for her, no one to love
her.

> 'Words of love Thy voice is speaking;
> "Come, come to Me."'

What was it made her think of that just now?
Was it not the Good Shepherd's voice, as he held
the poor lonely lamb closer to His bosom?

> 'Come, come to Me.'

'Good Shepherd, I do come,' said little weary
Rosalie; 'I come to Thee now!'

CHAPTER 12

A LONE LAMB

It was Sunday evening when the caravan reached the town where the fair was to be held. The travellers saw many churches and chapels open for evening service as they drove through the town. The gaily painted caravan looked strangely out of keeping with everything round it on that holy day.

Augustus met them as they came on the common which was apportioned to the show-people. It was a large waste piece of ground on a cliff overlooking the sea; for this great fair was held at a large watering-place on the sea-coast. The piece of ground which Augustus had selected was close to the beach, so that Rosalie could hear the rolling and dashing of the waves on the rocks below as she sat beside her mother that night. In the morning, as her mother was sleeping quietly, she stole out on the shore and wandered about among the rocks before the rest of the show-people were awake.

A long ridge of rocks stretched out into the sea, and Rosalie walked along this and watched the restless waves, as they dashed against it and broke into thick white foam. In some parts the rocky way was covered with small limpets, whose shells crackled under Rosalie's feet; then came some deep pools filled with green and red sea-weed, in which Rosalie discovered pink sea-anemones and restless little crabs. She examined one or two of these, but her heart was too sad and weary to be interested by them long, so she wandered on until she reached the extremity of the ridge of rocks. Here she sat for some time, gazing at the breakers, and watching the sunshine spreading over the silvery grey waters.

Several fishing-boats were already entering the harbour, laden with the spoils of the previous night, and Rosalie watched them coming in one by one and running quickly ashore. One of them passed close by the spot where the child was sitting. An old man and two boys were in it, and they were singing as they went by, in clear, ringing voices. Rosalie could hear the words of the song well, as she sat on the ridge of rocks:

'Last night, my lads, we toiled away,
    Oh! so drearily, drearily;
But we weighed our anchor at break of day,
    Oh! so cheerily, cheerily;
So keep up heart and courage, friends!
    For home is just in sight;
And who will heed, when safely there,
    The perils of the night?

'Just so we toil through earth's dark night,
    Oh! so wearily, wearily;
Yet we trust to sail at dawn of light,
    Oh! so cheerily, cheerily;
So keep up heart and courage, friends!
    For home is just in sight;
And who will heed, when safely there,
    The perils of the night?'

There was something in the wild tune, and something in the homely words, which soothed Rosalie's heart. As she walked back to the caravan she kept saying to herself:

> 'So keep up heart and courage, friends!
> For home is just in sight.'

'Just in sight, that must be for my mummy,' thought the child, 'and not for me; she is getting very near home!'

Her mother was awake when Rosalie opened the caravan door, but she seemed very weak and tired, and all that long day scarcely spoke. The child sat beside her, and tried to tempt her to eat, but she hardly opened her eyes, and would take nothing but a little water.

In the afternoon the noise of the fair began, the rattling of the shooting galleries, the bells of the three large roundabouts, and two noisy bands playing different tunes, and making a strange discordant sound, an odd mixture of the 'Mabel Waltz' and 'Poor Mary Ann.' Then as the crowds in the fair became denser, the shouts and noise increased on all sides, and the sick woman moaned to herself from time to time.

Augustus was far too busy preparing for the evening's entertainment to spend much time in the caravan. He did not know, or he would not see, that a change was passing over his wife's face, that she was even then standing on the margin of the river of death. And thus, about half an hour before the theatre opened, he called to Rosalie to dress herself for the play, and would listen to none of her entreaties to stay with her dying mother.

Her dying mother! Yes, Rosalie knew that it had come to that now. Child as she was, she could tell that there was something in her mother's face which had never been there before. Her eyes were opened to the truth at last, and she felt that death was not very far away.

How could she leave her! Her mother's hand was holding hers so tightly; her mother's eyes whenever they were opened were fixed on her so lovingly. How could she leave her mother even for an hour, when the hours which she might still have with her were becoming so few!

Yet Rosalie dared not stay. Was not this the great fair her father had been counting on all the year, and from which he hoped to reap the greatest profit? And had he not told her that very night, that if she broke down in her part in *this* town he would never forgive her as long as he lived?

No, there was no help for it; Rosalie must go. But not until the last moment—not until the very last moment, would she leave her dying mother. She dressed very quickly and sat down in her little white dress beside her mother's bed. Once more she held her mother's cold hand, and gently stroked her pale face.

'Little Rosalie,' said her mother, 'my darling, are you going—must you leave me?'

'Oh, mummy, mummy! it is so hard! So very, very hard!'

'Don't cry, my darling—my little lamb, don't cry! It's all right. Lift me up a little, Rosalie.'

The child altered her mother's pillows very gently, and then the sick woman whispered:

'I'm close to the deep waters; I can hear the sound of them now; it's the river of death, Rosalie; and I've got to cross it, but I'm not afraid; the Good Shepherd has laid me on His shoulder; and as I'm so very weak I think He'll carry me through.'

This was said with great difficulty; and when she had done speaking the dying woman's head fell back on the pillow.

Rosalie could not speak; she could only kiss her mother's hand and cry quietly as she watched. And then came her father's call to her to make haste and come into the theatre; and she had to disengage herself from her mother's hand, and, giving one last, long look, to shut the door and leave her—leave her alone.

What happened in the theatre that night Rosalie never exactly knew; it all seemed as a horrible dream to her. She said the words and acted her part; but she saw not the stage nor the spectators; her eyes all the time were on her mother's face, her hand all the time felt her mother's dying grasp. And yet, as she danced and sang, there were many there who thought her happy, many who envied her, and who would have gladly changed places with her. Oh, if they had only known; if they had only had the faintest idea of the anguish of that little heart, of the keen, cruel cutting sorrow with which it was filled!

Troubles some of these people undoubtedly had, cares and vexations and worries not a few, yet none of them had known anything of the heart-misery of that little actress: not one of them had ever been torn from the side of a dying mother and been compelled to laugh and sing when their very hearts were bleeding. From such soul-rending agony they had been saved and shielded; and yet they would have chosen the very lot which would have exposed them to it.

How very little they knew of what was going on behind the scenes; how little they guessed what a tumult of passionate sorrow was in little Rosalie's heart! So wild was her grief, that she hardly knew what she was doing, and after the play was over she could not have told how she had managed to get through it. Instead of going out on the platform, she darted swiftly out of the theatre and into her mother's caravan, almost knocking over several people who were passing by, and who stared at her in astonishment.

Her mother was not dead; oh, how glad Rosalie was for that! But she did not seem to hear her speak, and her breathing was very painful. Rosalie bent over her, and gave her one long, long kiss, and then hurried back into the theatre just as her father had missed her.

When she next came into the caravan all was still; her mother seemed to be sleeping more quietly, the painful breathing had ceased, and the child hoped she was easier. She certainly seemed more restful, and her hands were still warm, so she could not be dead, little Rosalie reasoned to herself.

Poor child! She did not know that even then she had no mother!

Weary and aching in every limb, little Rosalie fell asleep on the chair by her mother's side; and when she awoke with a shiver in the dead of night, and once more felt her mother's hand, it was as cold as ice. And Rosalie knew then that she was dead.

Trembling in every limb, and almost too startled to realize her sorrow, she unfastened the caravan door, and crept out into the darkness to tell her father. He and the men were sleeping soundly on the floor of the little theatre; and though Rosalie hammered against the gilded boards in front, she could make no one hear her. Again and again she knocked, but no answer came from within; for the theatre-people were tired with their night's work, and could not hear the little hands on the outside of the show. So the poor child had to return to the desolate caravan.

With one bitter cry of anguish, one long, passionate wail of grief, she threw herself on her mother's bed. Her sorrow could not disturb that mother now; she was gone to that land which is very far off, where even the sound of weeping is never heard. The Good Shepherd had carried her safely over the river, and, as Rosalie wept in the dark caravan, He was even then welcoming her mother to the home above; He was even then saying in tones of joy, yet more glad than before, 'Rejoice with Me, for I have found My sheep which was lost.'

Poor little desolate, motherless Rosalie! Had the Good Shepherd quite forgotten her? Was she left in her sorrow alone and forsaken? Was there no comfort for the orphaned lamb in her bitter distress? Did He pass her by untended and unblessed? Or did He not rather draw doubly near in that night of darkness? Did He not care for the lonely lamb?

Did He not whisper words of sweetest comfort and love to the weary, sorrowful Rosalie.

If not, what was it that made her feel, as she lay on her mother's bed, that she was not altogether deserted, that there was One who loved her still? What was it that gave her that strange, happy feeling that she was lying in the Good Shepherd's arms, and that He was folding her to His bosom even more tenderly than her mother had done? What was it, but the Good Shepherd fulfilling those gracious loving words of His: 'He shall gather the lambs with His arm and carry them in His bosom?'

It was the next morning. The sun had risen some time, and the show-people were beginning to stir; the fishing-boats were once more coming home, and the breakers were rolling on the shore. Augustus Joyce awoke with a strange feeling of uneasiness for which he could not account. Nothing had gone wrong the night before; Rosalie had made no mistake in her part, and his profits had been larger than usual. And yet Augustus Joyce was not happy. He had dreamed of his wife; and it was not often that he dreamed of her now. He had dreamed of her not as she was then, thin and worn, and wasted, but as she had been on his wedding-day, when she had been his bride, and he had promised to take her 'for better, for worse, for richer, for poorer, in sickness and in health, to love and to cherish her, till death should them part.'

Somehow or other, when Augustus woke, those words were ringing in his ears. What had he been to her in poverty? How had he treated her in sickness? Had he soothed her and cared for her,

and done all he could to make their burden press
lightly on her? Had he loved her and cherished
her? Loved her? What did those cruel words,
those bitter taunts, those unsympathizing speeches,
tell of the love of Augustus Joyce for his wife?
Cherished her? What kind of cherishing had he
bestowed on her during her illness? What kind
of cherishing had he shown her when he had
compelled her, almost fainting, to take her part
in the play?

'Till death us do part.' That time was very near
now. Augustus Joyce knew that. For once the
voice of conscience was heard by him. He could
not forget the lovely face he had seen in his dream,
nor the sad, reproachful gaze of those beautiful
dark eyes. He jumped from his bed and dressed
hastily. He would give his wife some kind words,
at least that morning. Conscience should not taunt
him with his bitter neglect again.

He hurried to the other caravan, opened the
door, and entered. What was the scene which
met his gaze?

The sunbeams were streaming in through the
small window, and falling on the bed. And there
lay his wife, so pale, so ghastly, so still, that Augustus
Joyce drew back in horror. And there, with her
arms round her mother's neck, and the wreath of
roses fallen from her hair on her mother's pillow,
lay little Rosalie, fast asleep, with the traces of
tears still on her cheeks. Intense weariness had
taken possession of her, and she had fallen asleep
on her mother's bed, in her white dress, just as she
had been acting at the play.

Augustus drew nearer to his wife, and sat down beside her. Yes, she was dead; there was no doubt of that. The kind words could never be spoken, she would never hear him again, he could never show his love to her now—never cherish her more. 'Till death us do part.' It *had* parted them now, parted them for ever. It was too late for Augustus Joyce to make any amends; too late for him to do anything to appease his conscience.

When Rosalie awoke, she found herself being lifted from the bed by her father, and carried into the other caravan. There he laid her on his own bed, and went out, shutting the door behind him.

The next few days seemed like one long dreary night to Rosalie. Of the inquest and the preparations for the funeral she knew nothing. She seemed like one in a dream. The fair went on all round her, and the noise and racket made her more and more miserable. What she liked best was to hear the dull roaring of the sea, after the lights were out and all in the fair was still.

For, somehow, with the roaring of the waves the fishermen's song came back to her:

> 'So keep up heart and courage, friends!
>   For home is just in sight;
> And who will heed, when safely there,
>   The perils of the night?'

Somehow—Rosalie hardly knew why—that song comforted and soothed her.

CHAPTER 13

VANITY FAIR

'Miss Rosie, dear, can I speak to you?' said Toby's voice, the day before the funeral.

'Yes; come in, Toby,' said the child, mournfully.

'I should like to see you, Miss Rosie,' said Toby, mysteriously; 'you won't be offended, will you? But I brought you this.'

Then followed a great fumbling in Toby's pockets, and from the depths of one of them was produced a large red pocket handkerchief, from which, when he had undone the various knots, he took out most carefully a little parcel, which he laid on Rosalie's knee.

'It's only a bit of black, Miss Rosie, dear,' he said. 'I thought you could put it on to-morrow; and you mustn't mind my seeing after it; there was no one to do it but me.'

Before Rosalie could thank him he was gone.

When she opened the parcel she found in it a piece of broad black ribbon—the best poor Toby could obtain. Rosalie's tears fell afresh as she fastened the ribbon on her hat, to be ready for the sorrowful service on the morrow.

The fair was nearly over, yet some of the shows lingered on, and there were still crowds of children round the roundabouts and shooting galleries when the mournful procession went by. The children at first drew back in astonishment; it was an unexpected sight, a coffin on the fair-ground. But astonishment soon gave way to curiosity, and they crowded round the little band of mourners and followed them nearly to the cemetery.

Augustus went through the service with an unmoved face. Conscience had been making its final appeal the last few days, and had made one last and mighty effort to arouse Augustus Joyce to repentance. But he had stifled conscience, suppressed it, trampled on it, extinguished it. God's Holy Spirit had been resisted and quenched already, and the conscience of the impenitent sinner was 'seared as with a hot iron'.

All the company of the theatre followed Augustus Joyce's wife to the grave, and more than one of them felt unusually moved as they looked at little sorrowful Rosalie walking by her father's side. She was quite calm and quiet, and never shed a tear until the service was over, and she was walking through the quiet cemetery a little behind the rest of the party. Then her eyes fell on Toby, who was walking near her with an air of real heartfelt sorrow on his honest face. He had tied a piece of crape round his hat, out of respect for his late mistress and for his mistress's little daughter.

Something in the curious way in which the crape was fastened on, something in the thought of the kindly heart which had planned this token of sympathy, touched Rosalie, and brought tears to her eyes for the first time on that sorrowful day.

For sometimes when a great sorrow is so strong as to dry up tears which would bring relief to the aching heart, a little thing, a very little thing, perhaps only a flower which our lost one loved, or something she touched for the last time or spoke of on the last day—or, it may be, as with Rosalie, only a spark of kindly sympathy where we have scarcely looked for it, and an expression of feeling which was almost unexpected—such a little thing as this will open in a moment the flood-gates of sorrow and give us that relief for which we have been longing and yearning in vain.

Rosalie found it like that; the moment her eyes rested on Toby's face and on Toby's bit of crape, she burst into a flood of tears, and was able to weep out the intenseness of her sorrow. And after that came a calm in her heart; for, somehow, she felt as if the angels' song was not yet over, as if they were still singing for joy over her mother's soul, and as if the Lord, the Good Shepherd, were still saying: 'Rejoice with Me, for I have found My sheep which was lost.'

They left the seaport town, and set off for a distant fair. Little Rosalie was very solitary in her caravan; everywhere and in everything she felt a sense of loss. Her father came occasionally to see her; but his visits were anything but agreeable, and she always felt relieved when he went away again to the other caravan. Thus the hours by day seemed long and monotonous, with no one inside the caravan to speak to, no one to care for or to nurse. She often climbed beside Toby and watched him driving, and spoke to him of the things which they passed by the way. But the hours by night were the longest of all, when the caravan was drawn up on a lonely moor or in a thickly-wooded valley; when Rosalie was left alone through those long desolate hours, and there was no sound to be heard but the hooting of the owls and the soughing of the wind among the trees. Then indeed little Rosalie felt desolate; and she would kneel on one of the boxes, and look out towards the other caravans, to be sure that they were near enough to hear her call to them if anything happened. Then she would kneel down and repeat her evening prayer again and again, and entreat the Good Shepherd to carry her in His arms, now that she was so lonely and had no mother.

They soon arrived at the fair for which they were bound, the acting went on as usual, and Rosalie had once more to take her place on the stage.

Very dreary and dismal and tawdry everything seemed to her. Her little white dress, the dress in which she had lain by her mother's side, was soiled and tumbled, and the wreath of roses looked crushed and faded, as Rosalie took it from the box. There was no mother to fasten it on her hair, no mother to cheer and comfort her as she went slowly up the theatre steps. Her father was looking for her, and told her they were all waiting, and then the play commenced.

Rosalie's eyes wandered up and down the theatre, and she wondered how it was that when she was a very little girl she had thought it so beautiful. It was just the same now as it had been then. The gilding was just as bright, the lamps were just as sparkling, the scenery had been repainted, and was even more showy and striking. Yet it all looked different to Rosalie. It seemed to her very

poor and disappointing and paltry, as she looked
at it from her place on the stage.

Then she thought of her mother, and of the
different place in which she was spending that very
evening. Rosalie had been reading about it that
afternoon before she dressed herself for the play.
She thought of the streets of gold on which her
mother was walking—pure gold, not like the tinsel
and gilt of the theatre; she thought of the white
robe, clean and fair, in which her mother was
dressed, so unlike her little soiled frock; she thought
of the new song her mother was singing, so different
from the coarse, low songs that were being sung
in the theatre; she thought of the music to which
her mother was listening, the voice of harpers
harping with their harps, and she thought how
different it was from the noisy band close to her,
and from the clanging music which her father's
company was making. She thought too of the words
which her mother was saying to the Good Shepherd,
perhaps even then, 'Thou art worthy; for Thou
wast slain, and hast redeemed me to God by Thy
blood': how different were these words from the
silly, foolish, profane words she herself was repeating!

Did her mother think of her? Little Rosalie
wondered if she did! How often she longed to be
with her mother in the Golden City, instead of
in the hot, wearying theatre!

The weeks went on; fair after fair was visited;
her father's new play was repeated again and again,
till it seemed very old to Rosalie; the theatre was
set up and taken down, and all went on much as
usual.

There was no change in the child's life, except that she had found a new occupation and pleasure. And this was teaching Toby to read.

'Miss Rosie,' he had said, one day, 'I wish I could read the Testament!'

'Can't you read, Toby?'

'Not a word, missie; I only wish I could. I've not been what I ought to be, Miss Rosie; and I do want to be different. Will you teach me?'

And it came to pass that Rosalie began to teach poor Toby to read. After that she might often be seen perched on the seat beside Toby, with her Testament in her hand, pointing out one word after another to him as they drove slowly along. When Toby was tired of reading, Rosalie would read to him some story out of the Bible. The one they both loved best, and the one they read more often than any other, was the Parable of the Lost Sheep. Rosalie was never tired of reading that, nor Toby of hearing it.

There was one thing for which Rosalie was very anxious, and that was to meet little Mother Manikin again. At every fair they visited she looked with eager eyes for the 'Royal Show of Dwarfs'; but they seemed to have taken a different circuit from that of the theatre party, for fair after fair went by without Rosalie's wish being gratified. At length one afternoon, the last afternoon of the fair, Toby came running to the caravan with an eager face.

'Miss Rosie,' he said, 'I've just found the "Royal Show of Dwarfs." They're here, Miss Rosie; and as soon as I caught sight of the picture over the door, thinks I to myself, "Miss Rosie will be glad." So

I went up to the door and spoke to the conductor (they've got a new one, Miss Rosie), and he said they were going to-night, so I ran off at once to tell you—I knew you would like to see little Mother Manikin again.'

'Oh dear,' said the child. 'I am glad.'

'You'll have to go at once, Miss Rosie; they're to start to-night the moment the performance is over; they're due at another fair to-morrow.'

'How was it that you didn't see the show before, Toby?'

'I don't know how it was, Miss Rosie, unless that it's at the very far end of the fair, and I haven't happened to be down that way before. Now, Miss Rosie, dear, if you like I'll take you.'

'I daren't leave the caravan, Toby, and father has the key; it wouldn't be safe, would it, with all these people about?'

'No,' said Toby, as he looked down on the surging mass of people, 'I don't suppose it would; you'd have all your things stolen, Miss Rosie.'

'What shall I do?' said the child.

'Well, if you wouldn't mind going by yourself, Miss Rosie, I'll keep guard here.'

Rosalie looked rather fearfully at the dense crowd beneath her; she had never wandered about the fair, but had kept quietly in the caravan, as her mother had wished her to do so; she knew very little of what was going on in other parts of the ground.

'Where is it, Toby?' she asked.

'Right away at the other end of the field, Miss Rosie. Do you hear that clanging noise?'

'Yes,' said Rosalie, 'very well; it sounds as if all the tin trays in the town were being thrown on one another!'

'That's the Giant's Cave, Miss Rosie, where that noise is, and the Dwarf Show is close by. Keep that noise in your ears, and you will be sure to find it.'

So Rosalie left Toby in the caravan, and went down into the pushing crowd. It was in the middle of the afternoon, and the fair was full of people. They were going in different directions, and it was hard work for Rosalie to get through them. It was only by very slow degrees that she could make her way through the fair.

It was a curious scene. A long row of bright gilded shows was on one side of her, and at the door of each stood a man addressing the crowd, setting forth the special merits and attractions of his show. First there were the waxworks with a row of specimen figures outside, and their champion proclaiming:

'Ladies and gentlemen, here is the most select show in the fair! Here is amusement and instruction combined! Here is nothing to offend the moral and artistic taste! You may see here Abraham offering up Isaac, and Henry IV in prison; Cain and Abel in the garden of Eden, and William the Conqueror driving out the ancient Britons!'

Then, as Rosalie pressed on through the crowd, she was jostled in front of the show of the Giant Boy and Girl. Here there was a great concourse of people, gazing at the huge picture of an enormously fat Highlander, which was hung over the

door. There was a curious band in front of this
show, consisting of a man beating a drum with
his right hand and turning a barrel organ with his
left, and another man blowing vociferously through
a trumpet. In spite of all this noise, a third man
was standing on a raised platform addressing the
crowds beneath:

'I say, I say! now exhibiting, the great Scottish
brother and sister, the greatest man and woman
ever exhibited! All for twopence; all for twopence! Children half-price! You're *just* in time,
you're in capital time; I'm so glad to see you in
such good time. Come now, take your seats, take
your seats!'

Rosalie struggled on, but another enormous
crowd stopped her way. This time it was in front
of the show of Marionettes, or dancing dolls. On
the platform outside the show was a man, shaking
a doll dressed as an iron-clad soldier.

'These are not living actors, ladies and gentlemen,' cried the man outside. 'If you come inside
you will see wonderfully artistic feats! None of
the figures are alive, which makes the performance
so much more interesting and pleasing. Now's
your chance, ladies and gentlemen! Now's your
chance! There's plenty of room! It isn't often
I can tell you so; it is the rarest occurrence; but
now there *is* nice room. Now's your chance!'

Past all these shows Rosalie pushed, longing to
get on, yet unable to hurry.

Then she came to a corner of the fair where a
Cheap Jack was crying his wares.

'Here's a watch,' said the man, holding it up,

'cost two pounds ten! I couldn't let you have it for a penny less! I'll give any one five pounds that will get me a watch like this for two pounds ten in any shop in the town. Come now, any one say two pounds ten?' giving a great slap on his knee. 'Two pounds ten; two pounds ten! Well, I'll tell you what; I'll take off the two pounds, I'll say ten shillings! Come, ten shillings! Ten shillings! Ten shillings! Well, I'll be generous, I'll say five shillings; I'll take off a crown. Come now, five shillings!' This was said with another tremendous slap on his knee. Then, without stopping a moment, he went from five shillings to four-and-sixpence, four shillings, three-and-sixpence. 'Well, I don't mind telling my dearest relation and friend, that I'll let you have it for two-and-six. Come now, two-and-six, two shillings, one-and-six, one shilling, sixpence. Come now, sixpence! Only sixpence!'

On this a boy held out his hand, and became for sixpence the possessor of the watch, which the man had declared only two minutes before he would not part with for two pounds ten shillings!

Rosalie pressed on and turned the corner. Here there was another row of shows; the Fat Boy, whose huge clothes were being paraded outside as an earnest of what was to be seen within; the Lady Without Arms, whose wonderful feats of knitting, sewing, writing, and tea-making were being rehearsed to the crowd; the Entertaining Theatre, outside which was a stuffed performing cat playing on a drum, and two tiny children, of about three years old, dressed up in the most extraordinary costumes, and dancing, with tambourines in their hands; the Picture Gallery, in which you could see Adam and Eve, Queen Elizabeth, and other distinguished persons: all these were on Rosalie's right-hand side and on her left was a long succession of stalls, on which were sold gingerbread, brandy-snap, nuts, biscuits, coco-nuts, boiled peas, hot potatoes, and sweets of all kinds. Here was a man selling cheap walking-sticks, and there another offering the boys a moustache and a pair of spectacles for a penny each, and assuring them that if they would only lay down the small sum of twopence they might become the greatest swells in the town.

How glad Rosalie was to get past them all, and to hear the clanging sound from the Giant's Cave growing nearer and nearer! And at last, to her joy, she arrived before the 'Royal Show of Dwarfs.' 'Now,' she thought, 'I shall see Mother Manikin.'

The performance was just about to begin, and the conductor was standing at the door inviting people to enter.

'Now, miss,' he said, turning to Rosalie, 'now's your time; only a penny, and none of them more than three feet high! Showing now! Showing now!'

Rosalie paid the money, and pressed eagerly into the show. The little people had just appeared, and were bowing and paying compliments to the company. But Mother Manikin was not there. Rosalie's eyes wandered up and down the show, and peered behind the curtain at the end, but Mother Manikin was nowhere to be seen. Rosalie could not watch the performance, so anxious was she to know if her dear little friend were within. At last the entertainment was over, and the giant and dwarfs shook hands with the company before ushering them out. Rosalie was the last to leave, and when the tall thin giant came up to her she looked up timidly into his face and said:

'Please, sir, *may* I see Mother Manikin?'

'Who are you, my child?' said the giant, majestically.

'I'm Rosalie, sir,—little Rosalie Joyce; don't you remember that Mother Manikin sat up with my mother when she was ill?'

The child's lips quivered as she mentioned her mother.

'Oh dear me! yes, I remember it; of course I do,' said the giant.

'Of course, of course,' echoed the three little dwarfs.

'Then please will you take me to Mother Manikin?'

'With the greatest of pleasure, if she were here,' said the giant with a bow; 'but the unfortunate part of the business is that she is *not* here!'

'No, she's not here,' said the dwarfs.

'Oh dear! oh dear!' said the child, with a little cry of disappointment.

'Very sorry, indeed, my dear,' said the giant. 'I'm afraid *I* shan't do as well.'

'No,' said Rosalie, mournfully, 'it was Mother Manikin I wanted; she knew all about my mother.'

'Very sorry indeed, my dear,' repeated the giant.

K

'Very sorry, very sorry!' re-echoed the dwarfs.

'Where is Mother Manikin?' asked the child.

'Why, the fact is, my dear, she has retired from the concern. Made her fortune, you see. At least, having saved a nice sum of money, she determined to leave the show. Somehow, she grew tired of entertaining company, and told us "old age must have its liberties".'

'Then where is she?' asked Rosalie.

'She has taken two little rooms in a town in the south of the county; very comfortable, my dear, you must call and see her some day.'

'Oh dear!' said little Rosalie; 'I'm so very, very sorry she is not here!'

'Poor child!' said the giant, kindly.

'Poor child! poor child!' said the dwarfs, as kindly.

Rosalie turned to go, but the giant waved her back.

'A glass of wine, Susannah!' he said.

'Yes, a glass of wine,' said Master Puck and Miss Mab.

'Oh no,' said the child; 'no thank you, not for me.'

'A cup of tea, Susannah!' called the giant.

'Oh no,' said Rosalie; 'I must go. Toby is keeping guard for me; I mustn't stay a minute.'

'Won't you?' said the giant, reproachfully; 'then good-bye, my dear. I wish I could escort you home; but we mustn't make ourselves too cheap, you know. Good-bye, good-bye!'

'Good-bye, my dear; good-bye!' said Master Puck and Miss Mab.

Rosalie sorrowfully turned homewards, and struggled out through the surging mass of people. The conductor at the door pointed out to her a shorter way to the theatre caravan. She was glad to get out of the clanging sound of the Giant's Cave, from the platform of which a man was assuring the crowd that if only they would come to this show they would be sure to come again that very evening, and would bring all their dearest friends with them.

Then the child went through a long covered bazaar, in which was a multitude of toys, wax dolls, wooden dolls, china dolls, composition dolls, rag dolls, and dolls of all descriptions; together with wooden horses, donkeys, elephants, and every kind of toy in which children delight. After this she came out on a more open space, where a Happy Family was being displayed to an admiring throng. It consisted of a large cage fastened to a cart, which was drawn by a comfortable-looking donkey. Inside the cage were various animals, living on the most friendly terms with each other—a little dog, in a smart coat, playing with several small white rats; a monkey hugging a little white kitten; a white cat, which had been dyed a brilliant yellow, superintending the sports of a number of mice and dormice; and a duck, a hen, and a guinea-pig, which were conversing together in one corner of the cage. Over this motley assembly was a board which announced that this Happy Family was supported entirely by voluntary contributions; and a woman was going about among the crowd shaking a tin plate at them, and crying out against their stinginess if they refused to contribute.

Rosalie passed the Happy Family with difficulty, and made her way down another street in the fair. On one side of her were shooting-galleries making deafening noise, and on the other were all manner of contrivances for making money. First came machines for the trial of strength, consisting of a flat pasteboard figure of some distinguished person, holding on his chest a dial-plate, the hand of which indicated the amount of strength possessed by any one who hit a certain part of the machine with all his might.

'Come now, try your strength!' cried the owner of one of these machines. 'I believe you're the strongest fellow that has passed by to-day! Come now, let's see what you can do!'

The required penny was paid, and there followed a tremendous blow, a tinkling of bells on the pasteboard figure, and an announcement from the owner of the show of the number of stones which the man had moved.

Then there were the weighing machines, armchairs covered with red velvet, in which you were invited to sit and be weighed; there was the sponge-dealer, a Turk in a turban, who confided to the crowd, in broken English, not only the price of his sponges, but also many touching and interesting details of his personal history. There was also the usual gathering of professional beggars, some without arms and legs, others deaf, or dumb, or blind, or all three, who go from fair to fair and town to town, and get so much money that they make five or six shillings a day, and live in luxury all the year round.

The child went quickly past them all, and came to the region of roundabouts, four or five of which were at work, and were whirling in different directions, and made her feel so dizzy that she hardly knew where she was going.

Oh! how glad she was to see her own caravan again—to get safely out of the restless, noisy multitude, out of the sound of the shouting of the show-people, the swearing of the drunken men and women, and out of the pushing and jostling of the crowd. She thought to herself as she went up the caravan steps, that if she had her own way, she would never go near a fair again; and oh! how she wondered that the people who *had* their own way came to it in such numbers.

Toby was looking anxiously for her from the caravan window.

'Miss Rosie, dear,' he said, 'I thought you were never coming; I got quite frightened about you; you're such a little mite of a thing to go fighting your own way in that great big crowd.'

'Oh, Toby,' said Rosalie, 'I haven't seen Mother Manikin!' and she told him what she had heard from the giant of Mother Manikin's prospects.

'I am sorry,' said Toby. 'Then you have had all your walk for nothing?'

'Yes,' said the child; 'and I never mean to go through the fair again if I can possibly help it— never again!'

CHAPTER 14

BETSEY ANN

THERE was still some time before Rosalie need dress herself for the play. She sat still after Toby had left her, thinking over all she had seen in the fair; and it made her very sad indeed. There were such a number of lies being told—she knew there were; such a number of things were being passed off for what they really were not. And then, after all, even if the shows were what they pretended to be, what a poor miserable way it seemed of trying to be happy! The child wondered how many in that moving multitude were really happy.

Rosalie was thinking about this when she heard a sound close to her, a very different sound from the shouting of the cheap-jacks or the noisy proclamations of the showmen. It was the sound of singing. She went to the door of the caravan and looked out. The little theatre was set up at the edge of the fair. Close to the street, and very near the caravan—so near that Rosalie could hear all they said—was standing a group of men. One of them had just given out a hymn, and he and all the rest were singing it. The child could hear every word of it distinctly. There was a chorus at the end of each verse, which came so often, that before the hymn was finished she knew it quite perfectly:

'Whosoever will, whosoever will;
Sound the proclamation over vale and hill;
'Tis a loving Father calls His children home;
Whosoever will may come!'

By the time they had finished the first verse of
the hymn a great crowd had collected round the
men, attracted perhaps by the contrast between
that sweet, solemn hymn and the din and tumult in
every other part of the fair.

Then one of the men began to speak:

'Friends,' he said—and as he spoke a great
stillness fell on the listening crowd—'Friends, I
have an invitation for you to-night; will you listen
to my invitation? You are being invited in all
directions to-night. Each man invites you to his
own show, and tells you that it is the best one in
the fair. Each time you pass him he calls out to you,
"Come! Come! Come now! Now's your time!"

'I too have an invitation for you to-night. I too
would say to you, "Come! Come! Come now!
Now's your time!" Jesus Christ, my friends, has
sent me with this invitation to you. He wants you
to *come*. He says, "*Come* unto Me, all ye that labour
and are heavy laden." He wants you to come *now*.
He says, "Come *now*, let us reason together; though
your sins be as scarlet, they shall be as white as
snow; though they be red like crimson, they shall
be as wool." He says to you "Now is your time."
"Behold," He says, "now is the accepted time,
now is the day of salvation."

'My friends, this is the invitation; but it is a very
different one from the one that man is giving at
that show over there. What does he say to those

people who are listening to him just now? Does he say, "Here's my show; the door is open, any one who likes may walk in! there's nothing to pay"? Does he say that, my friends? Does he ever give his invitation in that way? No, my friends; he always follows up his "Come, come now! now's your time!" with some such words as these: "Only twopence; only twopence; only twopence to pay! Come now!" And, if you do not produce your twopence, will he let you in? If you are so poor that you have not twopence in the world, will he say to you, "Come, come now! now's your time"? No, my friends, that he will not.

'Now the Lord Jesus Christ invites you quite differently. He cries out! "Ho! every one that thirsteth, come. Come without money! Come without price! Whosoever will may come!" Yes, my friends, the words "Whosoever will" are written over the door which the Lord Jesus Christ wants you to enter. This is one way in which His invitation is quite different from that which the man is giving from the door of that show.

'We will sing another verse of the hymn, and then I will tell you the other great difference between the two invitations.'

So again they sang:

'Whosoever will, whosoever will;
Sound the proclamation over vale and hill;
'Tis a loving Father calls His children home;
Whosoever will may come.'

'My friends,' said the speaker, when the verse was finished, 'there was once in Russia a very curious palace. It was built of nothing but ice. The walls were ice, and the roof was ice, and all the furniture was ice. There were ice sofas, ice chairs, ice fireplaces, ice ornaments. The water was made different colours, and then frozen, so that everything looked real and solid. At night the palace was lighted up, and it shone and sparkled as if it were set with diamonds. Every one said, "What a beautiful palace!"

'But it did not last, my friends, it did not last. The thaw came, and the ice palace faded away; there was soon nothing left of it but a pool of dirty water. It was all gone; it was very fine for a time; but there was nothing solid in it, and it melted away like a dream.

'My friends, yonder in that fair is the world's ice-palace! It sparkles, it glitters, it looks very fine; but it isn't solid; it won't last. To-morrow it will all be over; it will have melted away like a dream. Nothing will be left but dust, and dirt, and misery. There will be many aching heads and aching hearts this time to-morrow.

'The world's grandest display is a very disappointing thing after all. And this is the second way in which the Lord Jesus Christ's invitation is so different from that of the man at that show-door. When the Lord Jesus Christ says "Come," He has always something good to give, something that is solid, something that will last, something that will not disappoint you. He has pardon to give you; He has peace to give you; He has heaven to give you. All these are good gifts, all these are solid; all these will last; not one of them will disappoint you.

'Will you come to Him, my friends? He calls to you "Come, come now; Now's your time! There's room now: there is plenty of room now! Yet there is room; to-morrow it may be too late!"

'Will you not come to Him to-night?

'Whosoever cometh need not delay;
Now the door is open; enter while you may;
Jesus is the true, the only living way;
    Whosoever will may come.

'Whosoever will, whosoever will;
Sound the proclamation over vale and hill;
'Tis a loving Father calls His children home;
    Whosoever will may come.'

'Rosalie,' said her father's voice, 'be quick and get ready'; and Rosalie had to close the caravan door and dress for the play. But the hymn and the sermon were treasured up in the child's heart, and were never forgotten by her.

That was the last fair which Augustus Joyce visited that year. The cold weather was coming on; already there had been one or two severe frosts, and the snow had come beating down the caravan chimney, almost extinguishing the little fire.

Augustus thought it was high time that he sought for winter quarters; and, having made an engagement in a low town theatre for the winter months, he determined to go to the town at once, and dismiss his company until the spring.

On the road to the town they passed many other caravans, all bound on the same errand, coming like swallows to a warmer clime.

Rosalie's father went first to an open space or stable-yard, where the caravans were stowed away for the winter. Here he left Rosalie for some time, while he went to look for lodgings in the town. Then he and the men removed from the caravans the things which they would need, and carried them to their new quarters. When all was arranged, Augustus told the child to follow him, and led the way through the town.

How Rosalie wondered to what kind of place she was going! They went down several streets, wound in and out of different squares and courts, and the child had to run every now and then to keep up with her father's long strides. At last they came to a winding street full of tall, gloomy houses, before one of which her father stopped and knocked at the door. Some ragged children, without shoes or stockings, were sitting on the steps, and moved off as Rosalie and her father came up.

The door was opened by a girl about fifteen years old, with a miserable, careworn face, and dressed in an untidy, torn frock, which had lost all its hooks, and was fastened with large pins.

'Where's your mistress?' said Augustus Joyce.

The girl led the way to the back of the house, and opened the door of a dismal parlour, smelling strongly of tobacco. Rosalie gazed round her at the dirty paper on the walls, at the greasy chair-covers and the ragged carpet, and was not favourably impressed with her new abode. There were some vulgar prints in equally vulgar frames hanging on the walls; a bunch of paper flowers, a strange mixture of pink and red, blue and green and orange, was standing on the table and several cheap periodicals were lying on the chairs, as if someone had just been reading them.

Then the door opened, and the mistress of the house entered. She was an actress, Rosalie felt sure of that the first moment she saw her; she was dressed in a faded, greasy silk dress, and she greeted her new lodgers with an overpowering bow.

She took Rosalie upstairs, past several landings, where doors opened and people peered out to catch a glimpse of the new lodger, to a little attic in the roof, which was to be Rosalie's sleeping-place. It was full of boxes and lumber, which the woman of the house had stowed there to be out of the way; but in one corner the boxes were pushed on one side, and a little bed was put up for the child to sleep on, and a basin was set on one of the boxes for her to wash in. Rosalie's own box was already there; her father had brought it up for her before she arrived, and she was pleased to find that it was still uncorded. There were treasures in that box which no one in that house must see!

The woman of the house told Rosalie that in a few minutes her supper would be ready, and that she must make haste and come downstairs. So the child hastily took off her hat and jacket, and went down the numerous stairs to a room in the front of the house, where tea was provided for those lodgers who boarded with the woman of the house.

The child was most thankful when the meal was over. The rude, coarse jests and noisy laughter of the company grated on her ears, and she longed to make her escape. As soon as she could, she slipped from her father's side and crept upstairs to her little attic. Here at least she could be alone and quiet. It was very cold, but she unfastened the box and took out her mother's shawl, which she wrapped tightly round her. Then she opened out her treasures, and stowed them away as best she could. She opened the locket, and looked at the sweet, girlish face inside, and oh, how she wished she was with her aunt Lucy! How would she ever be able to keep that locket safely? That was her next thought. There was no key to the attic door, nor was there a key to her box. How would she be sure, when she was out at the theatre, that the people of the house would not turn over the contents of her box?

It was clear that the locket must be hidden somewhere, for Rosalie would never forgive herself if, after her mother had kept it safely all those years, she should be the one to lose it. She sat for some time thinking how she should dispose of it, and then came to the conclusion that the only way would be to wear it night and day round her neck underneath her dress, and never on any account to let any one catch sight of it. It was some time before she could carry out this plan to her satisfaction. She tied the locket carefully up in a small parcel, in which she placed the precious letter which her mother had written to her aunt Lucy, and she concealed the packet inside her dress, tying it round her neck.

After this Rosalie felt more easy, and took out her little articles of clothing, and hung them on some nails which she found on the attic door.

Then she took from her pocket her own little Testament, and crept up to the window to read a few verses before it was too dark.

So the child opened her book and began to read: 'Casting all your care upon Him, for He careth for you'—those were the first words which met her eyes. She repeated them over and over again to herself, that she might be able to remember them when the attic was quite dark. And they seemed just the words she needed; they were the Good Shepherd's words of comfort which He whispered to the weary lamb on His bosom.

For, as the shadows grew deeper and the room became darker, Rosalie felt very lonely and miserable. Once she thought she would go downstairs to look for her father; but whenever she opened the door there seemed to be such a noise and clamour below that she did not like to venture; she felt as if her mother would have liked her to stay where she was. She could not read now, and it was very cold indeed in the attic. The child shivered from head to foot, and wondered if the long hours would ever pass away. At last she determined to get into bed, for she thought she should be warmer there, and hoped she might get to sleep; but it was still early, and sleep seemed far away.

Then Rosalie thought of her text, 'Casting all your care upon Him, for He careth for you.'

'"All *your* care,"—that means *my* care,' thought the weary child, 'my own care. "*All* your care"; *all*—all the care about losing my mummy, and about having to stay in this noisy house, and about having to go and act in that wicked theatre, and about having to take care of my locket and my letter.

'"Casting all your care upon *Him,*" that means my own Good Shepherd, who loves me so. I wonder what casting it on Him means,' thought weary Rosalie. 'How can I cast it on Him? If my mummy was here I would tell her all about it, and ask her to help me. Perhaps that's what I've got to do to the Good Shepherd; I'll try.'

Rosalie knelt up in bed and said, 'O Good Shepherd, please, here's a little lamb come to speak to you. Please I'm very lonely, and my mummy is dead, and I'm so afraid someone will get my locket; please keep it safe; and I'm so frightened in the dark in this wicked house: please take care of me. And don't let me get wicked. I want to love You, dear Good Shepherd, and I want to meet my mummy in heaven: please let me; and wash my sins in the blood of Jesus. Amen.'

Then Rosalie lay down again, and felt much happier; the pain at her heart seemed to be gone.

'He careth for you.' How sweet those last words of the text were! She had not her mother to care for her, but the Good Shepherd cared for her: He loved her; He would not let her go wrong.

Rosalie was thinking of this and repeating her text again and again, when she felt something moving on the bed, and something very cold touched her hand. She started back at first, but, in a moment, she found it was nothing but the nose of a little soft furry kitten, that had crept in through the opening of the door; for Rosalie had left her door a little ajar, that she might get a ray of light from the gas lamp on the lower landing. The poor little kitten was very cold, and the child felt that it was as lonely and dull as she was. She put it in a snug place in her arms and stroked it very gently, till the tiny creature purred softly with delight.

Rosalie did not feel so lonely after the kitten had come to her. She had been lying still for some time, when she heard a step on the stairs, and her father's voice called:

'Rosalie, where are you?'

'I'm in bed,' said little Rosalie.

'Oh! all right,' said her father; 'I couldn't find you. Good-night.'

Then he went downstairs, and the child was once more alone; she lay stroking the kitten, and wondering if she should ever get to sleep. It was the longest night she ever remembered; it seemed as if it would never be bed-time—at least the bed-time of the people downstairs; the talking and laughing still went on, and Rosalie thought it would never cease.

At last the weary hours went by, and the people seemed to be going to bed. Then the light on the landing was put out, and all was quite still. The kitten was fast asleep; and Rosalie at length followed its example, and dropped into a peaceful slumber.

She had been asleep a long, long time, at least so it seemed to her, when she woke up suddenly, and, opening her eyes, she saw a girl standing by her bedside with a candle in her hand, and looking at her curiously. It was the little servant girl who had opened the door for her and her father.

'What is it?' said Rosalie, sitting up in bed; 'is it time to get up?'

'No,' said the girl; 'I'm only just coming to bed.'

'Why, isn't it very late?' asked the child.

'Late! I should think it is late,' said the poor little maid; 'it's always late when I come to bed. I have to wash the pots up after all the others has gone upstairs; ay! but my back does ache to-night! Bless you! I've been upstairs and downstairs all day long.'

'Who are you?' said Rosalie.

'I'm kitchen-maid here,' said the girl; 'I sleep in the attic next you. What did you come to bed so soon for?'

'I wanted to be by myself,' said Rosalie; 'there was such a noise downstairs.'

'La! do you call *that* a noise?' said the girl; 'it's nothing to what there is sometimes; I thought they were pretty peaceable to-night.'

'Do you like being here?' asked the child.

'Like it!' said the girl. 'Bless you! did you say *like* it? I hate it; I wish I could die. It's nothing but work, work, scold, scold, from morning till night.'

'Poor thing!' said Rosalie; 'what is your name?'

'Betsey Ann,' said the girl, with a laugh; 'it isn't a very pretty name, is it?'

'No,' said the child; 'I don't like it very much.'

'They gave me it in the infirmary; I was born there, and my mother died when I was born, and

L

I've never had a bit of pleasure all my life; I wish I was dead!'

'Shall you go to heaven when you die?' asked Rosalie.

'La! bless you, I don't know,' said the girl; 'I suppose so.'

'Has the Good Shepherd found you yet?' asked the child; 'because if He hasn't, you won't go to heaven, you know.'

The girl stared at Rosalie with a bewildered air of amazement and surprise.

'Don't you know about the Good Shepherd?' asked the child.

'Bless you, I don't know anything,' said the girl; 'nothing but my A B C.'

'Shall I read to you about it; are you too tired?'

'No, not if it's not very long.'

'Oh, it's short enough; I've got my book under my pillow.'

Rosalie read the Parable of the Lost Sheep; and the girl put down her candle on one of the boxes and listened.

'It's very pretty,' she said, when Rosalie had finished, 'but I don't know what it means.'

'Jesus is the Good Shepherd,' said Rosalie; 'you know who He is, don't you, Betsey Ann?'

'Yes, He's God; isn't He?'

'Yes, and He loves you so much,' said the child.

'Loves me!' said Betsey Ann; 'I don't believe He does. There's nobody loves me, and nobody never did!'

'Jesus does,' said Rosalie.

'Well, I never!' said the girl. 'Where is He? what's He like?'

'He's up in heaven,' said Rosalie, 'and yet He's in this room now, and He does love you, Betsey Ann; I know He does.'

'How do you know? Did He tell you?'

'Yes; He says in this book that He loved you, and died that you might go to heaven; you couldn't have gone to heaven if He hadn't died.'

'Bless you! I wish I knew as much as you do,' said the girl.

'Will you come up here sometimes, and I'll read to you?' said Rosalie.

'La! catch missis letting me. She won't let me wink scarcely! I never get a minute to myself, week in week out.'

'I don't know what I can do then,' said Rosalie. 'Could you come on Sunday?'

'Bless you, Sunday! Busiest day in the week here; lodgers are all in, and want hot dinners!'

'Then I can't see a way at all,' said Rosalie.

'I'll tell you what,' said the girl; 'I'll get up ten minutes earlier, and go to bed ten minutes later, if you'll read to me out of that little book, and tell me about somebody loving me. Ten minutes in the morning and ten minutes at night: come, that will be twenty minutes a day!'

'That would be very nice!' said Rosalie.

'But I get up awful soon,' said Betsey Ann, 'afore ever there's a glimmer of light; would you mind being waked up then?'

'Oh, not a bit,' said Rosalie, 'if only you'll come.'

'I'll come safe enough,' said the girl. 'I like you!

She took up her candle and was preparing to depart, when she caught sight of the kitten's tail peeping out from Rosalie's pillow.

'La! bless you, there's that kit!'

'Yes,' said the child; 'we're keeping each other company, me and the kitten.'

'I should think it's glad to have a bit of quiet,' said Betsey Ann; 'it gets nothing but kicks all day long, and it's got no mother—she was found dead in the coal-cellar last week; it's been pining for her ever since.'

'Poor little thing!' said Rosalie; and she held it closer to her bosom; it was a link of sympathy between her and the kitten; they were both motherless, and both pining for their mother's love. She would pet and comfort that little ill-used kitten as much as ever she could.

Then Betsey Ann wished Rosalie good-night, took up her candle, and went to her own attic, dragging her shoes after her.

Rosalie fell asleep.

CHAPTER 15

LIFE IN THE LODGING-HOUSE

TRUE to her promise, Betsey Ann appeared in the attic the next morning at ten minutes to five. Poor girl, she had only had four hours' sleep, and she rubbed her eyes vigorously to make herself wide awake, before she attempted to wake Rosalie. Then she put down her candle on the box and looked at the sleeping child. She was lying with one arm under her cheek, and the other round the kitten. It seemed a shame to wake her; but the precious ten minutes were going fast, and it was Betsey Ann's only chance of hearing more of what had so roused her curiosity the night before; it was her only opportunity of hearing of someone who loved her.

And to be loved was quite a new idea. She had been fed, and clothed, and provided for, to a certain extent; but none in the whole world had ever done anything for Betsey Ann because they loved her; that was an experience which had never been hers. There had been a strange fascination to her in those words Rosalie had spoken the night before: 'He loves you so much,'—she must hear some more about it. She gave Rosalie's hand, the hand which was holding the kitten, a very gentle tap.

'I say,' she said, 'I say, the ten minutes are going!'

The sleepy child turned over, and said, dreamily, 'I'll come in a minute, father; have you begun?'

'No; it's me,' said the girl; 'it's me; it's Betsey Ann. Don't you know you said you would read to me? Bless me, I wish I hadn't waked you, you look so tired!'

'Oh yes, I remember,' said Rosalie, jumping up; 'I'm quite awake now; how many minutes are there?'

'Oh, seven or eight at most,' said Betsey Ann, with a nod.

'Then we mustn't lose a minute,' said the child, pulling her Testament from under her pillow.

'La! I wish I was a good scholar like you,' said Betsey Ann, as Rosalie quickly turned over the leaves, and found the verse she had fixed on the night before for her first lesson to the poor ignorant kitchen-maid.

'For ye know the grace of our Lord Jesus Christ, that though He was rich, yet for your sakes He became poor, that ye through His poverty might be rich.'

'Isn't that a beautiful verse?' said little Rosalie; 'I used to read it to my mummy, and she liked it so much.'

'Tell me about it,' said Betsey Ann; 'put it plain-like for me.'

'"Ye know,"' said Rosalie, 'that's how it begins. *You* don't know, Betsey Ann, but you will do soon, won't you?'

'La! yes,' said the girl, 'I hope I shall.'

'"Ye know the grace." I'm not quite sure what grace means; I was thinking about it the other day; and now my mummy's dead I've no one to ask about things; but I think it must mean love; it seems as if it ought to mean love in this verse; and He *does* love us, you know, Betsey Ann, so we can't be far wrong if we say it means love.

'"Ye know the love of our Lord Jesus Christ"— that's the One we talked about last night, the One who loves you, Betsey Ann; "That though He was rich," that means He lived in heaven, my mummy said, and had ever so many angels to wait on Him, and everything He wanted, all bright and shining. "Yet for your sakes," that means *your* sake, Betsey Ann, just as much as if it had said: "You know the love of the Lord Jesus Christ, that, though He was rich, yet for Betsey Ann's sake He became poor."'

'Well, I never!' said Betsey Ann.

'Poor,' repeated the child; 'so poor, my mummy said, that He hadn't a house, and had to tramp about from one place to another, and had to work in a carpenter's shop, and used to be hungry just like we are.'

'Well, I never!' said Betsey Ann; 'what ever did He do that for?'

'That's the end of the verse,' said Rosalie. '"That ye through His poverty might be rich." That is, He came to be poor and die, that you might be rich and go to live up where He came from— up in the City of Gold, and have the angels wait on you, and live with Him always up there.'

Betsey Ann opened her eyes wider and wider in astonishment. 'Well, now! I never heard the like!

Why didn't nobody never tell me nothink about it before?'

'I don't know,' said Rosalie; 'is the time up?'

'Very near,' said Betsey Ann, with a sigh. 'There's lots to do afore missis is up; there's all the rooms to sweep out, and all the fires to light, and all the breakfasts to set, and all the boots to clean.'

'Can you wait one minute more?' asked the child.

'Yes,' said Betsey Ann; 'bless you, I can wait two or three; I'll take off my shoes and run quick downstairs; that will save some time.'

'I wanted you just to speak to the Lord Jesus Christ before you go,' said Rosalie.

'*Me* speak to Him! Why, bless you, I don't know how!'

'Shall we kneel down?' said the child. 'He's in the room, Betsey Ann, though you can't see Him, and He'll hear every word we say.

'O Lord Jesus, please, we come to you this morning. Thank you very much for leaving the Gold City for us. Thank you for coming to be poor, and for loving us, and for dying for us. Please make Betsey Ann love you. Please save Betsey Ann. Please forgive Betsey Ann's sins. Amen.'

'I shall think about it all day; I declare I shall!' said Betsey Ann, as she took off her slipshod shoes and prepared to run downstairs. 'My word, I wonder nobody never told me afore!'

When Rosalie went downstairs that morning, she found her father and the woman of the house in earnest conversation in the parlour. They stopped talking when the child came into the room, and her father welcomed her with a theatrical bow.

'Good morning, madam,' he said; 'glad to find that you have benefited by your nocturnal slumbers.'

Rosalie walked up to the fire with the kitten in her arms, and the woman of the house gave her a condescending kiss, and then took no further notice of her.

It was a strange life for little Rosalie in the dirty lodging-house, with no mother to care for or to nurse, and with no one to speak kindly to her all day long but poor Betsey Ann.

Clatter, clatter, clatter, went those slipshod shoes, upstairs and downstairs, backwards and forwards, hither and thither. Sweeping, and dusting, and cleaning, and washing up dishes from morning till night, went Betsey Ann; and whenever she stopped a minute, her mistress's voice was heard screaming from the dingy parlour:

'Betsey Ann, you lazy girl! What are you after now?'

That afternoon, as Rosalie was sitting reading in her little attic, she heard the slipshod shoes coming upstairs, and presently Betsey Ann entered the room.

'I say,' she said, 'there's a young boy wants to speak to you below; can you come?'

Rosalie hastened downstairs, and found Toby standing in the passage, his hat in his hand.

'Miss Rosie, I beg pardon,' he said, 'but I've come to say good-bye.'

'Oh, Toby! are you going away?'

'Yes,' said Toby; 'master doesn't want us any more this winter; he's got no work for us; so he has sent us off. I'm right sorry to go, I'm sure I am.'

'Where are you going, Toby?'

'I can't tell, Miss Rosie,' said he, with a shrug of his shoulders; 'where I can get, I suppose.'

'Oh dear! *I am* sorry you must go,' said the child.

'I shall forget all my learning,' said Toby, mournfully; 'but I tell you what, Miss Rosie, I shall be back here in spring; master will take me on again, if I turn up in good time, and then you'll teach me a bit more, won't you?'

'Yes,' said Rosalie, 'to be sure I will; but, Toby, you won't forget everything, will you?'

'No, Miss Rosie,' said Toby, 'that I won't! It's always coming in my mind; I can't curse and swear now as I used to do; somehow the bad words seem as if they would choke me. The last time I swore (it's a many weeks ago now, Miss Rosie), I was in a great passion with one of our men, and out came those awful words, quite quick, before I thought of them. But the next minute, Miss Rosie, it all came back to me—all about the Good Shepherd, and how He was looking for me, and loving me, and I at that very time doing just what vexes Him. Well, I ran out of the caravan, and I tried to forget it; but somehow it seemed as if the Good Shepherd was looking at me quite sorrowful like; and I couldn't be happy, Miss Rosie, not until I'd asked Him to forgive me, and to help me never to do so no more.'

'I'm so glad, Toby!' said little Rosalie; 'If you love the Good Shepherd, and don't like to grieve Him, I think He must have found you, Toby.'

'Well, I don't know, Miss Rosie; I hope so, I'm sure. But now I must be off; only I couldn't go without bidding you "good-bye"; you've been so good to me, Miss Rosie, and taught me all I know.'

After this, Rosalie's life went on much the same from day to day. Every morning she was wakened by Betsey Ann's touch upon her hand, and she read and explained a fresh verse from the Testament to the poor little maid. Rosalie used to choose the verses the night before, and put a mark in the place, so that she might begin to read the moment she awoke, and thus not one of the ten minutes might be wasted. Betsey Ann always listened with opened mouth and eyes. And she did not listen in vain; a little ray of light seemed, after a time, to be breaking in on that poor, dark, neglected mind—a little ray of sunshine, which lighted up her dark, dismal life, and made even poor Betsey Ann have something worth living for. 'He loves me'; that was the one idea which was firmly fixed in her mind. 'He loves me so much that He died for me.' And that thought was enough to make even the dismal lodging-house and the hard life seem less dark and dreary than they had done before.

Slowly, very slowly, a change came over the girl, which Rosalie could not help noticing. She was gentler than she used to be, more quiet and patient. And she was happier too. She did not wish to die now, but seemed to be trying to follow the Good Shepherd, who had done so much for her.

These morning talks with Betsey Ann were the

happiest parts of Rosalie's days. She did not like the company she met in the large lodging-house; they were very noisy, and the child kept out of their way as much as possible. Many of them were actors and actresses, and were in bed till nearly dinner-time. So the morning was the quietest time in the lodging-house; even the woman of the house herself was often not up. Then Rosalie would sit with the kitten on her knee before the fire in the dingy parlour, thinking of her mother and of her aunt Lucy, and putting her hand every now and then inside her dress, that she might be quite sure that her precious locket and letter were safe.

The poor little kit had a happy life now. Rosalie always saved something from her own meals for the motherless little creature; many a nice saucerful of bread and milk, many a dainty little dinner of gravy and pieces of meat did the kitten enjoy. Every night when Rosalie went to bed it was wrapped up in a warm shawl, and went to sleep in the child's arms. Wherever Rosalie was to be found, the kitten was to be found also. It followed her upstairs and downstairs, it crept to her feet when she sat at meals, it jumped on her knee when she sat by the fire, it was her constant companion everywhere.

There was only one time when the kitten and Rosalie were separated, and that was when she went to perform in the theatre. Then it would scamper downstairs after her, watch her drive away, and wander restlessly about the house, crying until she returned.

No words can describe how much Rosalie disliked

going to the theatre now. It was a low, dirty place, and filled every evening with very bad-looking people. Rosalie went there night after night with her father; and the woman of the house, who was an actress in the same theatre, went with them. She was not unkind to Rosalie, but simply took no notice of her. To Rosalie's father she was very polite; she always gave him the best seat in the dingy parlour, and the chief place at table, and consulted his comfort in every possible way. Often when Rosalie came suddenly into the room, she found her father and the woman in earnest conversation, which was always stopped the moment that the child entered. And as they drove together to the theatre, many whispered words passed between them, of which Rosalie heard enough to make her feel quite sure that her father and this woman were on the best of terms.

Thus the weeks and months passed by, and the time drew near when the days would be long and light again, and her father's engagement at the theatre would end, and he would set out on his summer rounds to all the fairs in the country. Rosalie was eagerly looking forward to this time; she was longing to get out of this dark lodging-house; to have her own caravan to herself, where she might read and pray undisturbed; to breathe once more the pure country air; to see the flowers, and the birds, and the trees again; to see Toby, and to continue his reading-lessons. To all this Rosalie looked forward with pleasure.

Only Betsey Ann grew very mournful as the time drew near.

'La!' she would say, again and again, 'what ever shall I do without you? Who ever shall I find to read to me then?'

And then the slipshod shoes dragged more heavily at the thought, and the eyes of poor Betsey Ann filled with tears.

Yet she knew now that, even when Rosalie went away, the Good Shepherd loved her, and would be with her still.

CHAPTER 16

A DARK TIME

ONE morning when Rosalie was upstairs in her attic reading quietly to herself, the door opened softly, and Betsey Ann came in with a very troubled look on her face, and sat down on one of the boxes.

'What's the matter, Betsey Ann?' asked the child.

'Deary me, deary me!' said the girl; 'I'm real sorry, that I am!'

'What is it?' said Rosalie.

'If it only wasn't *her*, I shouldn't have minded so much,' explained Betsey Ann; 'but she is——. I can't tell you *what* she is; she's dreadful sometimes. Oh, dear, I *am* in a way about it!'

'About what?' asked Rosalie again.

'I've guessed as much a long time,' said Betsey Ann; 'but they was very deep, them two, and I couldn't be quite sure of it. There's no mistake about it now, more's the pity!'

'Do tell me, please, Betsey Ann!' pleaded the child.

'Well, Rosalie,' said the girl, 'I may as well tell you at once. You're going to have a ma!'

'A what?' said the child.

'A ma; a new mother; *she's* going to be Mrs. Augustus Joyce.'

'Oh, Betsey Ann!' said Rosalie, mournfully; 'are you sure?'

'Sure! yes,' said the girl, 'only too sure; one of the lodgers told me, and, what's more, them two have gone off together just now; and it's my belief that they've gone to church to finish it off. Ay, but I am sorry!'

'Oh, Betsey Ann!' sobbed little Rosalie; 'what *shall* I do?'

'I never was so cut up about anything,' said the girl; 'she's been just decent to you till now; but when she's made it fast she'll be another woman, you'll see! Oh dear! Oh dear! But I must be off; I've lots to do afore she comes back, and I shall catch it if I waste my time. Oh, Rosalie! I wish I hadn't told you,' she added, as she listened to the child's sobs.

'Oh, it's better I should know,' said Rosalie; 'thank you, dear Betsey Ann!'

'I'm real sorry, I am!' said the girl as she went downstairs. 'I'm a great strong thing, but she's such a weakly little darling; I'm real sorry, I am!'

When Betsey Ann was gone, Rosalie was left to her own sorrowful meditations. All her dreams of quiet and peace in the caravan were at an end. They would either remain in the large lodging-house, or, if they went on their travels, the woman of the house would be also the woman of the caravan. And how would she ever be able to keep her dear letter and locket safe from those inquisitive eyes?

What a wretched life seemed before the child as she looked on into the future! She seemed further from her aunt Lucy than ever before. And how would she ever be able to do as her mother had asked her—to read her Bible, and pray, and learn more and more about the Good Shepherd?

Life seemed very dark and cheerless to little Rosalie. The sunshine had faded from her sky, and all was chill and lifeless. She lost hope and she lost faith for a time. She thought the Good Shepherd must have forgotten all about her to let this new trouble come to her. She was very much afraid that she would grow up a bad woman, and never, never, never see her mother again.

When she had cried for some time, and was becoming more and more miserable every moment, she stretched out her hand for her little Testament, to see if she could find anything there to comfort her. She was quickly turning over the leaves, not knowing exactly where to read, when the word *sheep* attracted her attention.

Ever since the old man had given her the picture, she had always loved those texts the best which speak of the Lord as the Shepherd and His children as the sheep. This was the one on which her eyes fell that sorrowful day:

'My sheep hear My voice, and I know them, and they follow Me: and I give unto them eternal life, and they shall never perish neither shall any man pluck them out of My hand.'

These words seemed to soothe and comfort the troubled child, even before she had thought much about them. But when she began to think the verses over word by word, as was her custom, they seemed to Rosalie to be everything she wanted just then.

'"My sheep." It's the Good Shepherd speaking,' thought Rosalie, 'speaking about His sheep. "*My*

M

sheep," He calls them. Am I one of them? I *hope*
I am. I *have* asked the Good Shepherd to find me,
and I think He has.

'"My sheep hear My voice." O please, Good
Shepherd,' said little Rosalie, 'may I hear Your
voice; may I do all that You tell me, and always
try to please You!

'"And I know them." I'm glad the Good
Shepherd knows me,' said Rosalie; 'because if He
knows me, and knows all about me, then He knows
just how worried and troubled I am. He knows
all about father getting married, and the woman
coming to live in our caravan; and He knows how
hard it is to do right when I've only bad people
round me; yes, He knows all that.

'"My sheep hear My voice, and I know them,
and they follow Me." "They follow Me." Where
the Good Shepherd goes the sheep go,' said Rosalie
to herself. 'He walks first and they walk after;
they go just where He went. Oh dear, I'm sure I
don't think He ever went to fairs or theatres or
shows. And I *must* go; can I be a sheep after all?
But then I don't want to go; I don't like going a
bit. As soon as ever I can I won't go any more.
And the Good Shepherd must know that if He
knows His sheep. And I do want to follow Him,
to walk after Him, and only say and do what the
Good Shepherd would have said and done. I do
hope I *am* a little sheep, though I do live in a
caravan.'

The second verse seemed to Rosalie even more
beautiful than the first: 'I give unto them eternal
life.'

She knew what *eternal* meant; it meant for ever and for ever; her mother had taught her that. And this was the Shepherd's present to His sheep. Eternal life; they were to live for ever and ever. It was a wonderful thought; Rosalie's little mind could not quite grasp it, but it did her good to think of it. It made present troubles and worries seem very small and insignificant. If she was going to live for ever, and ever, and ever, what a little bit of that long time would be spent in this sorrowful world! All the troubles would soon be over. She would not have to live in a caravan in heaven; she would never be afraid there of doing wrong, or growing up wicked. Oh, that was a very good thought! The sorrow would not last always; good times were coming, for Rosalie had received the Good Shepherd's present, even eternal life.

'And they shall never perish, neither shall any man pluck them out of My hand.'

'After all,' thought Rosalie, 'that is the very sweetest bit of all the text. If I am one of the sheep, and if I am in the Good Shepherd's hand, no one can pluck me out of it. What a strong hand He must have to hold all His sheep so fast!'

'O Good Shepherd,' prayed Rosalie again, 'hold me fast; don't let any one pluck me out of Thy hand, not father, not the new mother, nor any of the people here. Please hold me very tight; I am so afraid, I'm only a little sheep, and I have no one to help me, so please hold me tighter than the rest. Amen.'

Oh, how this prayer lightened little Rosalie's heart! She rose from her knees comforted. Safe in the Good Shepherd's hand, who or what could harm her?

It was well she had been thus strengthened and comforted, for a few minutes afterwards she heard her father's voice calling her, and going downstairs, she found him sitting in the parlour with the woman of the house.

'Rosalie,' said her father, with a theatrical bow, 'allow me to introduce you to your new mother!'

He evidently expected her to be very much astonished, but Rosalie tried to smile, and gave her hand to the woman of the house. And, as she put her little trembling hand in that of her new mother, it seemed to Rosalie as if the Good Shepherd tightened the hold of *His* hand on His little forlorn lamb.

Her father, after a few heartless remarks about Rosalie having a mother again, dismissed her, and she went up again to her attic.

The very next day Rosalie saw clearly that Betsey Ann's predictions were likely to be fulfilled.

'Rosalie,' said her stepmother, as soon as she came downstairs, 'I intend that you shall make yourself useful now. I'm not going to have a daughter of mine idling away her time as you have been doing lately. Fetch some water and scour the sitting-room floor. When you've done that, there's plenty more for you to do! *I* know how to make girls work.'

Rosalie thought she could very easily believe that.

Her father was standing by, and only laughed at what his wife said.

'It will do her good,' Rosalie heard him say, as she went out of the room; 'she wants a bit of hard work.'

And a bit of hard work Rosalie certainly had; it was difficult to say whether she or Betsey Ann had the more to do. Perhaps Rosalie's life was the harder, for every night she had to go, weary and footsore as she was, to the theatre and take her usual part in the play. And when she came home at night she was so worn out that she could hardly drag herself up to the attic to bed.

The hard work was not what Rosalie minded most. There was fault-finding from morning till night, without one single word of praise or encouragement; there were unkind, cruel words, and even blows to bear. But what was worse than all these, was that the child had to wait on many of the rude and noisy lodgers, and heard and saw much, very much that was so bad and unholy, that the very thought of it made her shudder as she knelt at night to pray in her little attic.

Would she ever be kept from harm in this dreadful place? Sometimes little Rosalie felt as if she would sink under it; but the Good Shepherd's hand was round her, and she was kept safe; no one could pluck her out of that hand. No evil thing could touch her; the Good Shepherd's little sheep was perfectly safe in His almighty grasp.

Rosalie saw very little of her father at this time. He was out nearly all the afternoon, only coming home in time to go with them to the theatre at night; and then when the performance was over he often did not go home with his wife and Rosalie but sent them and went with one of his friends in another direction. Where they went Rosalie never knew; she feared it was to one of the gin-palaces which stood at the corner of almost every street in that crowded neighbourhood.

Rosalie never knew when her father returned home. He had a latchkey, and let himself in after all in the house were asleep; and Rosalie saw him no more until dinner-time the next day, when he would come downstairs in a very bad temper with every one.

She was often unhappy about him, and would have done anything she could to make him think about his soul. But it seemed of no use speaking to him; ever since his wife's death he appeared quite hardened, as if he had buried his last convictions of sin in her grave. Augustus Joyce had resisted the Spirit of God; and that Spirit seemed to strive with him no longer. The Good Shepherd had longed and yearned to find him; but the wayward wanderer had refused to hear His voice: he had preferred the far country and the wilderness of sin to the safe fold and the Shepherd's arms. He had hardened his heart to all that would have made him better, and for the last time had turned away from the tender mercies of God!

One night when Rosalie had gone to bed, with the kitten beside her on the pillow, and had fallen asleep from very weariness and exhaustion, she was startled by a hand laid on her shoulder, and Betsy Ann's voice saying:

'Rosalie, Rosalie! what can it be?'

She started up quickly, and saw Betsey Ann standing beside her, looking very frightened.

'Rosalie,' she said, 'didn't you hear it?'

'Hear what?' asked the child.

'Why, I was fast asleep,' said Betsey Ann, 'and I woke all of a minute, and I heard the doorbell ring.'

'Are you sure?' said Rosalie; 'I heard nothing.'

'No,' said Betsey Ann; 'and missis doesn't seem to have heard; every one's been asleep a long time; but then you see I have to go so fast to open it when it rings in the day, I expect the sound of it would make *me* jump up if I was ever so fast asleep.'

'Are you quite sure, Betsey Ann?' said Rosalie once more.

She had hardly spoken the words before the bell rang again very loudly, and left no doubt about it.

'Do you mind coming with me, Rosalie?' said Betsey Ann, as she prepared to go downstairs.

'No, not at all,' said the child; 'I'm not afraid.'

The two girls hastily put on their clothes and went downstairs. Just as they arrived at the bottom of the steep staircase, the bell rang again, louder than before, and the woman of the house came on the landing to see what it was.

'Please, ma'am,' said Betsey Ann, 'it's the house-bell; me and Rosalie are just going to open the door.'

'Oh! it's nothing, I should think,' said she: 'it will be someone who has arrived by the train, and has come to the wrong door.'

While they were talking the bell rang again, more violently than before, and Betsey Ann opened the door. It was a dark night, but she could see a man standing on the doorstep.

'Is this Mrs. Joyce's?' he inquired.

'Yes,' said the girl; 'she lives here.'

'Then she's wanted,' said the man; 'tell her to be quick and come.'

'What's the matter?' asked Rosalie.

'It's an accident,' said the man; 'he's in the hospital, is her husband; he's been run over by a van. I'll take her there if she'll be quick; I'm a mate of Joyce's, and I was passing at the time.'

Rosalie stood as if she had been stunned, unable to speak or move, while Betsey Ann went upstairs to tell her mistress.

'It's all along of that drink,' said the man, more as if talking to himself than to Rosalie. 'It's an awful thing is drink; he never saw the van nor heard it, but rolled right under the wheels. I was passing by, I was, and I said to myself, "That's Joyce." So I followed him to the infirmary, and came to tell his wife. Dear me, it's a bad job, it is!'

In a few minutes Mrs. Augustus Joyce came downstairs dressed to go out. Rosalie ran up to her and begged to go with her, but she was ordered to go back to bed, and her stepmother hastened out with the man.

What a long night that seemed to Rosalie! How she longed for morning to dawn, and lay awake straining her ears for any sound which might tell her that her stepmother had returned.

At length as the grey morning light was stealing into the room, the doorbell rang again, and Betsey

Ann went to open the door for her mistress. Rosalie felt as if she did not dare to go downstairs to hear what had happened.

Presently the slipshod shoes came slowly upstairs, and Betsey Ann came into the attic.

'Tell me,' said the child, 'what is it?'

'He's dead,' said Betsey Ann, solemnly; 'he was dead when she got there; he never knew nothing after the·wheels went over him. Isn't it awful though?'

Little Rosalie could not speak, and could not cry; she sat quite still and motionless.

What of her father's soul? That was the thought uppermost in her mind. Oh, where was he now? Was his soul safe? Could she have any hope, even the faintest, that he was with her mother in the bright home above?

It was a terrible end to Augustus Joyce's ungodly and sinful life. Cut off in the midst of his sins, with no time for repentance, no time to take his heavy load of guilt to the Saviour, whose love he had scorned and rejected. Oh! how often had he been called and invited by the Good Shepherd's voice of love, but he would not hearken, and now it was too late.

CHAPTER 17

ALONE IN THE WORLD

IT was the day after her father's funeral. Rosalie was busily engaged sweeping the staircase, when her stepmother came out of the dingy parlour, and called to the child to come down.

As soon as Rosalie entered the room, Mrs. Joyce told her to shut the door, and then asked her in a sharp voice, how long she intended to stop in her house.

'I don't know, ma'am,' said Rosalie, timidly.

'Then you ought to know,' returned Mrs. Joyce; 'I suppose you don't expect me to keep you, and do for you. You're nothing to me, you know.'

'No,' said Rosalie; 'I know I'm not.'

'I thought I'd better tell you at once,' she said, 'that you might know what to expect. I'm going to speak to the institution about you; that's the best place for you now; they'll make you like hard work, and get a good place for you, like Betsey Ann.'

'Oh no,' said Rosalie, quickly; 'no, I don't want to go there.'

'Don't want!' repeated Mrs. Joyce; 'I dare say you don't want; but beggars can't be choosers, you know. If you'd been a nice, smart, strong girl, I might have kept you instead of Betsey Ann; but a little puny thing like you wouldn't be worth her salt; no, no, miss; your fine days are over; to the Institution you'll go, sure as I'm alive.'

'Please, ma'am,' began Rosalie, 'my mother, I think, had some relations——'

'Rubbish, child!' said her step-mother, interrupting her; 'I never heard of your mother having any relations; I don't believe she had any, or if she had, they're not likely to have anything to say to you. No, no; the institution is the place for you, and I shall take care you go to it before you're a day older. Be off now, and finish the stairs.'

'Betsey Ann,' said Rosalie, as they went upstairs together that night, long after every one else in that large house was fast asleep, 'Betsey Ann, dear Betsey Ann, I'm going away!'

'La! bless me!' said Betsey Ann; 'what do you say?'

'I'm going away to-morrow, dear!' whispered Rosalie, 'so come into my attic, and I'll tell you all about it.'

The two girls sat down on the bed, and Rosalie told Betsey Ann what her stepmother had said to her, and how she could not make up her mind to go into the institution, but had settled to leave the lodging-house before breakfast the next morning, and never to come back any more.

'Rosalie,' said Betsey Ann, 'what ever will you do? You can't live on air, child; you'll *die* if you go away like that!'

'Look here,' said Rosalie, in a very low whisper, 'I can trust you, Betsey Ann, and I'll show you something.'

She put her hand in her bosom, and brought out a little parcel, and when she had opened it she handed the locket to Betsey Ann.

'La, how beautiful!' said the girl; 'I never saw it before.'

'No,' said Rosalie; 'I promised my mummy I would never lose it; and I've been so afraid lest someone should see it and take it from me.'

'Who ever is this pretty little woman, Rosalie?'

'She's my mummy's sister. Oh, such a good kind woman! That is her picture when she was quite young; she is married now, and has a little girl of her own. So now I'll tell you all about it,' said Rosalie. 'Just before my mummy died, she gave me that locket, and she said if ever I had an opportunity I was to go to my aunt Lucy. She wrote a letter for me to take with me, to say who I am, and to ask my aunt Lucy to be kind to me.

'Here's the letter,' said the child, taking it out of the parcel; 'that's my mummy's writing:

> "MRS. LESLIE,
> "Melton Parsonage."

'Didn't she write beautifully?'

'Well but, Rosalie,' said Betsey Ann, 'what do you mean to do?'

'I mean to go to my aunt Lucy, dear, and give her the letter.'

'*She'll* never let you go, Rosalie; it's no use trying; she said you should go to the institution, and she'll keep her word.'

'Yes, I know she'll never give me leave,' said Rosalie; 'so I'm going to-morrow morning before breakfast. She doesn't get up till eleven, and I shall be far away then.'

'Rosalie, do you know your way?'

'No,' said the child wearily; 'I shall have to ask, I suppose. How far is Pendleton from here, Betsey Ann, do you know?'

'Yes,' said Betsey Ann; 'there was a woman in the institution came from there; she often told us of how she walked the distance on a cold snowy day; it's fourteen or fifteen miles, I think.'

'Well, that's the town,' said Rosalie, 'where the old man gave me my picture; and it was the first village we passed through after that, where my aunt Lucy lived. Melton must be about five miles farther than Pendleton.'

'Oh, Rosalie!' said Betsey Ann, 'that's near upon twenty miles! You'll never be able to walk all that way!'

'Oh yes,' said the child; 'I must try; because if once I get there—oh, Betsey Ann, just think, if once I get there, to my own dear aunt Lucy!'

Betsey Ann buried her face in her hands, and began to sob.

'La, bless you, it's all right!' she said, as Rosalie tried to comfort her; 'you'll be happy there, and it will be all right. But, oh dear me, to think I've got to stay here without you!'

'Poor Betsey Ann!' said the child, as she laid her little hand on the girl's rough hair; 'what can I do?'

'Oh, I know it's all right, Rosalie; it's better than seeing you go to the institution; but I didn't think it would come so soon. Can't you tell the Good Shepherd, Rosalie, and ask Him to look after *me* a bit, when you're gone?'

'Yes, dear,' said the child; 'let us tell Him now.'

They knelt down, hand in hand, on the attic floor, and Rosalie prayed:

'O Good Shepherd, I am going away; please take care of Betsey Ann, and comfort her, and help her to do right, and never let her feel lonely or unhappy. And please take care of me, and bring me safe to my aunt Lucy. And if Betsey Ann and I never meet again in this world, please may we meet in heaven! Amen.'

Then they rose from their knees comforted, and began to make preparations for Rosalie's departure.

She would take very little with her, for she had so far to walk that she could not carry much. She filled a very small bag with the things that she needed most; and wrapped her little Testament up, and put it in the centre, with the small pair of blue shoes which had belonged to her little brother. Her picture, too, was not forgotten, nor the card with the hymn on it. When all was ready, they went to bed: but neither of them could sleep much that night.

As soon as it was light, Rosalie prepared to start. She wrapped herself in her mother's warm shawl, for it was a raw, chilly morning, and took her little bag in her hand. Then she went into Betsey Ann's attic to say good-bye.

'What am I to tell the missis, when she asks where you've gone?' said the girl.

'You can say, dear, that I've gone to my mother's relations, and am not coming back any more. She won't ask any more, if you say that: she'll only be too glad to get rid of me. But I'd rather she didn't know where my aunt Lucy lives; so don't say anything about it, please, Betsey Ann, unless you're obliged.'

The girl promised, and then with many tears they took leave of each other.

Just as Rosalie was starting, and Betsey Ann was opening the door for her, she caught sight of something very black and soft under the child's large shawl.

'La, bless me!' she cried; 'what's that?'

'It's only the poor little kit,' said Rosalie; 'I couldn't leave her behind. She took a piece of fish the other day, and the mistress was so angry, and is going to give her poison. She said last night she would poison my kit to-day. She called out after me, as I went out of the room, "Two pieces of rubbish got rid of in one day: to-morrow *you* shall go to the institution, and that wretched little thief of a kitten shall be poisoned." And then she laughed, Betsey Ann. So I couldn't leave my dear little kit behind, could I?' and Rosalie stroked its black fur very lovingly as she spoke.

'But how will you ever carry it, Rosalie? It won't be good all that way, rolled up like that.'

'Oh, I shall manage, dear; it will walk a bit when we get in the country: it follows me just like a dog!'

'What are you going to eat on the way, Rosalie? Let me fetch you a bit of something out of the pantry.'

'Oh no, dear!' said Rosalie decidedly; 'I won't take anything, because it isn't mine. But I have a piece of bread that I saved from breakfast, and I have twopence which my father gave me once, so I shall manage till I get there.'

Then Rosalie went out into the great world alone; and Betsey Ann stood at the door to watch her go down the street. Over and over again did Rosalie come back to say good-bye, over and over again did she turn round to kiss her hand to the poor little servant girl, who was watching her down the street. And then when she turned the corner and could no longer see Betsey Ann's friendly face, Rosalie felt really alone. The streets looked very wide and dismal then, and Rosalie felt that she was only a little girl, and had no one to take care of her. She looked up to the blue sky, and asked the Good Shepherd to help her, and to bring her safely to her journey's end.

It was about six o'clock when Rosalie started; the men were going to their work, and were hurrying quickly past her. Rosalie did not like to stop any of them to ask them the way; they seemed too busy to have time to speak to her. She ventured timidly to put the question to a boy of fifteen, who was sauntering along whistling with his hands in his pockets; but he only laughed, and asked her why she wanted to know. So Rosalie walked on, very much afraid that after all she might be walking in the wrong direction. She next asked some children on a doorstep; but they were frightened at being spoken to, and ran indoors.

Then Rosalie went up to an old woman who was opening her shutters, and asked her if she would be so very good as to tell her the way to Pendleton.

'What, my dear?' said the old woman; 'speak up! I'm deaf!'

Though Rosalie stood on tiptoe to reach up to her ear, and shouted again and again, she could not make the old woman hear, and at last had to give it up, and go on her way. She was feeling very lonely now, poor child, not knowing which way to turn, or to whom to go for help. True, there were many people in the street, but they were walking quickly along, and Rosalie was discouraged by her unsuccessful attempts, and afraid to stop them. She had come some way from the street in which she had lived with her stepmother, and had never been in this part of the town before. She was feeling very faint and hungry, from having come so far before breakfast; but she did not like to eat her one piece of bread, for she would need it so much more later in the day. But she broke off a small piece, and gave it to the poor hungry little kit, which was mewing under her shawl.

'Oh,' thought Rosalie, 'if only I had someone to help me just now—someone to show me where to go, and what to do!'

There was a story which the child had read in her little Testament, which came suddenly into her mind just then. It was a story of the Good Shepherd when He was on earth. The story told how He sent two of His disciples into the city of Jerusalem to find a place for Him and them, where they might eat the Passover. The two men did not know to which house to go; they did not know who, in the great city of Jerusalem, would be willing to give a room. But Jesus told them that as soon

N

as they came inside the city gate they would see a man walking before them. He told them the man would be carrying a pitcher of water; and that when they saw this man, they were to follow him, and go down just the same streets as he did. He told them that by-and-by the man would stop in front of a house, and go into the house, and then when they saw him go in, they were to know that that was the right house, the house in which they were to eat the Passover.

Rosalie remembered this story now, as she stood at the corner of a street, not knowing which way to turn. How she wished that a man with a pitcher of water would appear, and walk in front of her, that she might know which way to go! Though she looked up and down the street, she saw no one at all like the man in the story. There were plenty of men, but none of them had pitchers, nor did they seem at all likely to guide her into the right way.

But the Good Shepherd was the same, Rosalie thought—as kind now as He was then—so she spoke to Him in her heart, in a very earnest little prayer.

'O Good Shepherd, please send me a man with a pitcher of water to show me the way, for I am very unhappy, and I don't know what to do. Amen.'

CHAPTER 18

THE LITTLE PITCHER

ROSALIE had shut her eyes as she said her little prayer; and when she opened them she saw before her a little girl about five years old, in a very clean print frock and white pinafore, with a pitcher in her hand. Rosalie almost felt as if she had fallen from heaven. She was not a man, to be sure, and the pitcher was filled full of milk, and not water, yet it seemed very strange that she should come up just then.

The little girl was gazing up into Rosalie's face, and wondering why she was shutting her eyes. As soon as Rosalie opened them she said:

'Please will you open our shop door for me? I'm afraid of spilling the milk.'

Rosalie turned round, and behind where she was standing was a very small shop. In the window were children's slates, and slate-pencils, with coloured paper twisted round them, and a few wooden tops, and balls of string, and little boxes of ninepins, and a basket full of marbles, and pink and blue shuttle-cocks. It was a very quiet little shop indeed, and it looked as if very few customers ever entered it. The slate pencils and battledores and marbles looked as if they had stood in exactly the same places long before the little girl was born.

Rosalie lifted the latch and opened the door of the little shop for the child to go in. And the little pitcher went in before her.

Rosalie felt sure she must follow it, and that here she would find some one to tell her the way.

'Popsey,' said a voice from the next room, 'little Popsey, is that you?'

'Yes, granny,' said the child, 'and I've not spilt a drop—not one single drop, granny.'

'What a good, clever little Popsey!' said granny, coming out of the back parlour to take the milk from the child's hands.

'Please, ma'am,' said Rosalie, seizing the opportunity, 'would you be so very kind as to tell me the way to Pendleton?'

'Yes, to be sure,' said the old woman; 'you're not far wrong here; take the first turn to the right, and you'll find yourself on the Pendleton Road.'

'Oh, thank you very much,' said Rosalie; 'is it a very long way to Pendleton, please, ma'am?'

'Ay, my dear,' said the old woman; 'it's a good long step—Popsey, take the milk in to grandfather, he's waiting breakfast—it's a good long way to Pendleton, my dear, maybe fourteen or fifteen miles.'

'Oh dear! that sounds a very long way!' said Rosalie.

'Who wants to go there, my dear?' asked the old woman.

'I want to go,' said Rosalie, sorrowfully.

'*You* want to go, child! Why, who are you going with? and how are you going? You're surely not going to walk?'

'Yes I am,' said Rosalie; 'thank you, ma'am; I must walk as fast as I can.'

'Why, you don't look fit to go, I'm sure,' said the

old woman, 'such a poor little, weakly thing as
you look! What ever is your mother about, to
let you go?'

'I haven't got a mother!' said Rosalie, bursting
into tears; 'she's dead, is my mother. I haven't
got a mother any more.'

'Don't cry, my poor lamb!' said the old woman,
wiping her eyes with her apron. 'Popsey hasn't
got a mother neither: her mother's dead—she lives
with us, does Popsey. Maybe your grandmother
lives in Pendleton; does she?'

'No,' said Rosalie; 'I'm going to my mother's
sister, who lives in a village near Pendleton. I was
to have gone to the institution to-day, but I think,
perhaps, she'll take care of me, if I only can get
there.'

'Poor lamb!' said the old woman; 'what a way
you have to go! Have you had your breakfast
yet? You look fit to faint!'

'No,' said Rosalie; 'I have a piece of bread in my
bag, but I was keeping it till I got out of the town.'

'Jonathan,' called out the old woman, 'come
here.'

Rosalie could hear a chair being pushed from
the table on the stone floor in the kitchen, and the
next moment a little old man came into the shop
with spectacles on his nose, a blue handkerchief
tied round his neck, and a black velvet waistcoat.

'Look ye here, Jonathan,' said his wife, 'did
you ever hear the like? Here's this poor lamb
going to walk all the way to Pendleton, and never
had a bite of nothing all this blessed day; what
do you say to that, Jonathan?'

'I say,' said the old man, 'that breakfast's all ready, and the coffee will be cold.'

'Yes; so do I, Jonathan,' said the old woman; 'so come along, child, and have a sup before you start.'

The next minute found Rosalie seated by the round table in the little back kitchen with a cup of steaming coffee and a slice of hot cake before her. Such a cosy little kitchen it was, with a bright fire burning in the grate, and another hot cake standing on the top of the oven, to be kept hot until it was wanted. The fire-irons shone like silver, and everything in the room was as neat and clean and bright as it was possible for them to be.

Popsey was sitting on a high chair between the old man and woman, and the pitcher of milk was just in front of her; she had been pouring some of it into her grandfather's coffee.

The old man was very attentive to Rosalie, and wanted her to eat of everything on the table. He had heard what she had told the old woman in the shop, for the kitchen was so near that every word could be heard distinctly.

Before Rosalie would eat a morsel herself she said, looking up in the old woman's face, 'Please, ma'am, may my little kit have something to eat? it's so very, very hungry.'

'Your little kit!' exclaimed the old woman; 'why, what do you mean, child, where is it?'

The kitten answered this question by peeping out from the child's shawl. They were all very much astonished to see it; but when Rosalie told its story, and the old woman heard that it was

motherless, like Popsey, it received a warm welcome.
The pitcher of milk was emptied for the hungry
kitten, and when its breakfast was over it sat purring
in front of the bright fire.

It was a very cosy little party, and they all
enjoyed themselves very much. Rosalie thought
she had never tasted such good cakes nor drunk
such delicious coffee. Popsey was delighted with the
kitten, and wanted to give all her breakfast to it.

When breakfast was over, Popsey got down from
her high chair and went to a chest of drawers,
which stood in a corner near the fireplace. It was
a very old-fashioned chest of drawers, and on the
top of it were arranged some equally old-fashioned
books. In the middle of these was a large well-
worn family Bible.

Popsey put a chair against the chest of drawers
and standing on tiptoe on it, brought down the
Bible from its place. It was almost as much as
she could lift, but she put both her arms round
it and carried it to her grandfather. The old
man cleared a space for it on the table, and laid
it before him. Then looking up at the old woman
he said:

'Are you ready, grandmother?'

To which the old woman answered: 'Yes,
Jonathan, quite ready'; and pushed her chair a
little way from the table, and folded her arms.
Rosalie followed her example and did the same.
Popsey had seated herself on a wooden stool at
her grandfather's feet.

Then there was a pause, in which the old man
took an extra pair of spectacles from a leathern

case, fixed them on his nose, and turned over the leaves of his Bible. And then, when he had found his place, he began to read a psalm. The psalm might have been chosen on purpose for Rosalie; she almost started when the old man began:

'The Lord is my Shepherd: I shall not want.'

That was the first verse of the psalm: and it went on to tell how the Shepherd leads His sheep into green pastures, and makes them to lie down beside still waters: and how the sheep need fear no evil, for He is with them. His rod and His staff they comfort them.

When he had finished reading, the old man offered a very suitable little prayer, in which Rosalie and Popsey were both named, and committed to the Shepherd's care.

Then, when they rose from their knees, Rosalie felt it was high time she should go on her journey. But the old woman would not hear of her going till she had wrapped up all that was left of the cake in a little parcel, and slipped it into the child's bag. After this, they all three—the old man, the old woman, and Popsey—went to the door to see Rosalie start.

Popsey could hardly tear herself from the kitten, and the old woman could not make up her mind to stop kissing Rosalie. But at length the good-byes were over, and the child set off once more on her travels, feeling warmed and comforted and strengthened.

It was about eight o'clock now, so there was no time to lose. She easily found the Pendleton Road, and the old man had directed her when she found it to go straight on, turning neither to the right hand nor to the left, till she reached Pendleton itself. She would pass through several villages, he said, but she was not to turn aside in any direction. So Rosalie had no further anxiety about the way she was to go. All she had to do was to walk along as quickly as possible.

The first part of the road lay through the outskirts of the town; on either side of the way were rows of red-brick houses and small shops, and every now and then a patch of field or garden.

By degrees the houses and shops became fewer, and the patches of field and garden became more numerous.

After a time, the houses disappeared altogether, and there was nothing on both sides of the road but fields and gardens.

The sun was shining now, and the hedges were covered with wild roses. Over Rosalie's head there was a lark singing in mid-air, and by the side of the path grew the small pink flowers of the wild convolvulus. Rosalie could not help stopping to gather some sprays of this, and to twist them round her hat. It was so many months since she had seen any flowers; and they brought the old days back to her, when Toby used to put her down from the caravan, that she might gather the flowers for her mother.

For the first few miles Rosalie enjoyed her walk very much, everything was so bright and pleasant. Every now and then she put the kitten on the ground, and it ran by her side.

Then the child sat on a bank and ate the cake

which Popsey's grandmother had given her. And the little black kit had Benjamin's share of the little entertainment.

As the day went on the poor little kit became tired, and would walk no more; and Rosalie grew tired also. Her feet went very slowly now, and she felt afraid that night would come on long before she reached Pendleton. Then the sun was hidden by clouds, and wind began to sweep through the trees, and blew against the child, so that she could hardly make any way against it.

Rain came, only a few drops at first, then quicker and quicker, till Rosalie's shawl became wet through and her clothes clung heavily to her ankles. Still on she walked, very heavily and wearily, and the rain poured on, and the kitten shivered under the shawl. Rosalie did her very best to keep it warm, and every now and then she stroked its wet fur, and spoke a word of comfort to it.

Wearily the child's little feet pressed on, as they struggled against the cold and piercing wind!

How would she ever reach the town? How would she ever hold on till she arrived at her aunt Lucy's?

CHAPTER 19

SKIRRYWINKS

ROSALIE was almost in despair, almost ready to give up and sit down by the roadside, when she heard a sound behind her. It was the rumbling sound of wheels, and in another minute Rosalie saw coming up to her two large caravans, so like the caravan in which she used to travel with her mother, that the child felt as if she were dreaming as she looked at them.

The caravans were painted a brilliant yellow, just as her father's caravans used to be; and there were muslin curtains and pink bows in the little windows, just like those through which she had so often peeped.

When the caravans came up to Rosalie she saw a woman standing at the door of the first one, talking to the man who was driving.

The woman caught sight of the child as soon as they overtook her.

'Holloa!' she called out, 'where are you off to?'

'Please,' said Rosalie, 'I'm going to Pendleton, if only I can get there.'

'Give her a lift, John Thomas,' said the woman; 'give the child a lift; it's an awful day to be struggling along against wind and storm.'

'All right,' said John Thomas, pulling up; 'I've no objections, if the lass likes to get in.'

Rosalie was very grateful indeed for this offer, and climbed at once into the caravan.

The woman opened the door for her, and took off her wet shawl as she went in.

'Why! you've got a kitten there,' she said as she did so; 'wherever are you taking it to? It's half-drowned with the rain.'

'Yes, poor little kit!' said Rosalie; 'I must try to dry it—it is so cold!'

'Well, I'll make a place for both of you near the fire,' said the woman, 'if only my children will get out of the way.'

Rosalie looked in vain for any children in the caravan; but the woman pointed to a large black dog, a pigeon, and a kitten, which were sitting together on the floor.

'Come, Skirrywinks,' said the woman, addressing herself to the kitten, 'come to me.'

As soon as she said 'Skirrywinks,' the kitten, which had appeared to be asleep before, lifted up its head and jumped on her knee. The great black dog was ordered to the other end of the caravan, and the pigeon perched on the dog's head.

The woman gave Rosalie a seat near the little stove, and the child warmed her hands and dried and comforted her poor little kitten. No words can tell how thankful she was for this help on her way. She felt sure that John Thomas must be a man with a pitcher of water, sent to help her on her journey.

For some time the woman leant out of the caravan, continuing her conversation with her husband, and Rosalie was able to look about her. The inside of

the caravan was very like that in which she had been
born, and had lived so many years. There was a
little cooking stove, just like that which her mother
had used; and in the corner was a large cupboard
filled with cups and saucers and plates, just like
the one which Rosalie herself had arranged so often.
But what struck her more than anything else was
that on the side of the caravan was nailed up her
picture, the picture of the Good Shepherd and the
sheep!

It was exactly the same picture, and the same text
was underneath it:

'Rejoice with Me; for I have found My sheep
which was lost. There is joy in the presence of the
angels of God over one sinner that repenteth.'

Rosalie could not help feeling in her bag to be
sure that her own picture was safe, so precisely
did the picture on the wall resemble it.

The picture seemed to have hung there for some
time, for it was very smoky and discoloured, but
still it looked very beautiful, Rosalie thought, and
her eyes filled with tears as she gazed at it. Oh,
how it brought her mother's dream to her mind,
and carried her thoughts away from the caravan
to the home above, where even now, perhaps, her
mother was being called by the Good Shepherd
to rejoice with Him over some sheep which was
lost, but which the Good Shepherd had found
again!

When the woman put her head into the caravan
she began to talk to Rosalie, to ask her where she
had come from, and where she was going, and what
she was going to do. She seemed a friendly woman,

though she spoke in a rough voice. All the time she was talking, Skirrywinks was sitting on her shoulder and the pigeon on her head. Rosalie's kitten seemed afraid of the large black dog, and crept into the child's arms.

When they had chatted together for some time, Rosalie ventured to mention the picture, saying that it seemed so strange to see it here, for that she had one exactly like it.

'Oh! have you?' said the woman; 'that's Jinx's picture; an old man gave it to him just a year ago, it will be; it was at Pendleton fair.'

'Why! that's where I got mine,' said Rosalie; 'it must be the same old man.'

'I should say it was,' said the woman; 'he came to the caravans on a Sunday afternoon.'

'Oh yes! it's the same old man,' said Rosalie. 'I have my picture here, in my bag. I wouldn't ever part with it.'

'Wouldn't you?' said the woman; 'well, I don't believe Jinx would. He nailed it up that very Sunday, and there it's been ever since.'

'Who's Jinx?' asked Rosalie.

'He's our boy; at least he lives with us. Me and John Thomas haven't got any children of our own, so we keeps a few. There's Jinx, he's chief of them; and then there's Skirrywinks, and Tozer, and Spanco, and then there's Jeremiah—you haven't seen Jeremiah; he's in bed, you'll see him when Jinx comes.'

'Where is Jinx?' asked Rosalie, almost expecting he would turn out to be some kind of animal which was hidden away in a corner of the caravan.

'Oh, he's in the next van, with Lord Fatimore,' said the woman; 'he'll be here soon, when it's time for these young people to be fed and trained. He's very clever, is Jinx; you never saw any one so clever in all your life. I'll be bound he can make 'em do anything. We might just as well shut up, if we hadn't Jinx. He's a deal more popular than Lord Fatimore is—folks say they never saw such a sight as when Jeremiah and Skirrywinks dance the polka together; and it's all Jinx that has taught them.'

In about half an hour the caravans were stopped, and the wonderful Jinx arrived. He was very short, not taller than Rosalie; he was so hump-backed, that he seemed to have no neck at all; and he had a very old and wizened and careworn face. It was hard to tell whether he was a man or a boy, he was so small in stature, and yet so sunken and shrivelled in appearance!

'Jinx,' said the woman as he entered, 'here's a young girl come to your performance.'

'Most happy, miss,' said Jinx, with a bow.

The moment that he came into the caravan, Skirrywinks and the dog sat on their hind legs, and the pigeon alighted on his head. As soon as he spoke, Rosalie heard a noise in a basket behind her as of something struggling to get out.

'I hear you, Jeremiah,' said Jinx; 'you shall come, you shall.'

He took the basket, and put his hand inside.

'Now, Jeremiah,' he said, 'now, Jeremiah, if I can find you, Jeremiah, come out, and show the company how you put on your new coat.'

Out of the basket he brought a hare, which was wonderfully tame, and allowed itself to be arrayed in a scarlet jacket.

Jinx made all the animals go through their several performances, after which each received his proper share of the mid-day meal. But Skirrywinks seemed to be Jinx's favourite; long after the others were dismissed she sat on his shoulders, watching his every movement.

'Well, what do you think of them?' he said, turning to Rosalie when he had finished.

'They're very clever,' said the child, 'very clever indeed!'

'That kit of yours couldn't do as much,' said Jinx, looking scornfully at the kitten which lay in Rosalie's lap.

'No,' said the child; 'but she's a very dear little kit, though she doesn't jump through rings nor dance polkas.'

'Well, tastes differ,' said Jinx; 'I prefer Skirry-winks.'

'You've got a picture like mine,' said Rosalie, after a time, when she saw that Jinx seemed inclined to talk.

'Yes,' he said; 'have you one like it? I got it at Pendleton fair.'

'So did I,' said Rosalie; 'the same old man gave one to me. Has *He* found *you*, Mr. Jinx?' said Rosalie, in a lower voice.

'*Who* found me? What do you mean?' said Jinx, with a laugh.

'Why, haven't you read the story about the picture?' said the child. 'It says where it is underneath.'

'No, not I,' said Jinx, laughing again; 'thinks I, when the old man gave it to me, it's a pretty picture, and I'll stick it on the wall; but I've never troubled my head any more about it.'

'Oh, my mother and I—we read it nearly every day,' said Rosalie; 'it's such a beautiful story!'

'Is it?' said Jinx; 'I should like to hear it; tell it to me; it will pass the time as we go along.'

'I can read it if you like,' said Rosalie. 'I have it here in a book.'

'All right! read on,' said Jinx, graciously.

Rosalie took her Testament from her bag; but before she began to read Jinx called out to the woman, who was leaning out of the caravan talking to her husband.

'Old mother!' he called out, 'come and hear the little 'un read; she's going to give us the history of that there picture of mine. You know nothing about it, I'll be bound.'

Jinx was wrong, for when Rosalie had finished reading, the woman said, 'That will be the Bible you read out of. I've read that often when I was a girl. I went to a good Sunday-school then.'

'Don't you ever read it now?' said Rosalie.

'Oh, I'm not so bad as you think,' said the woman, not answering her question; 'I think of all those things at times. I'm a decent woman in my way. I know the Bible well enough, and there's a many a *deal worse* than I am!'

'If you would like,' said Rosalie, timidly, 'I'll find it for you in your Bible, and then you can read it again, as you used to do when you were a girl.'

o

The woman hesitated when Rosalie said this.

'Well, to tell you the truth, I haven't got my Bible here,' she said; 'my husband sent all the things we wasn't wanting at the time to his relations in Scotland; and somehow the Bible got packed up in the hamper; it will be a year since now. I was very vexed about it at the time.'

'Has the Good Shepherd found you, ma'am?' asked the child.

'Oh, I don't know, child; I don't want much finding; I'm not so bad as all that; I'm a very decent woman, I am. John Thomas will tell you that.'

'Then I suppose,' said Rosalie, looking very puzzled, 'you must be one of the ninety and nine.'

'What do you mean, child?' asked she.

'I mean one of the ninety and nine sheep which don't need any repentance, because they were never lost; and the Good Shepherd never found them, nor carried them home, nor said of them, "Rejoice with Me, for I have found My sheep which was lost."'

'Well,' said Jinx, looking at Rosalie, with a half-amused face, 'if the old mother's one of the ninety and nine, what am I?'

'I don't know,' said Rosalie, gravely; 'you must know better than I do, Mr. Jinx.'

'Well, how is one to know?' he answered; 'if I'm not one of the ninety and nine, what am I then?'

'Do you really want to know?' said the child, gravely; 'because if not, we won't talk about it, please.'

'Yes,' said Jinx, in quite a different tone; 'I really do want to know about it.'

'My mother said one day,' said Rosalie, 'that she thought there were only three kinds of sheep in the parable. There are the ninety and nine sheep who were never lost, and who need no repentance, because they've never done anything wrong nor said anything wrong, but have always been quite good, and holy, and pure; that's *one* kind. My mother said she thought the ninety and nine must be the angels; she didn't think there were any in this world.'

'Hear that, old mother?' said Jinx; 'you must be an angel, you see. Well, little 'un, go on.'

'Then there are the lost sheep,' said Rosalie, 'full of sin, and far away from the fold; they don't love the Good Shepherd, and sometimes they don't even know that they *are lost*. They are very far from the right way—very far from being perfectly good and holy.'

'Well,' said Jinx, 'and what's the *third* kind of sheep?'

'Oh, that's the sheep which was lost, but is found again!'

'What are they like?' asked the lad.

'They love the Good Shepherd; they listen to His voice, and follow Him, and never, never want to wander from the fold.'

'Is that *all* the kinds?' asked Jinx.

'Yes,' said Rosalie, 'that's all.'

'Well,' said Jinx, thoughtfully. 'I've made up my mind which I am.'

'Which, Mr. Jinx?' asked the child.

'Well,' he said, 'you see I can't be one of the ninety and nine, because I've done lots of bad things in my life. I've got into tempers, and I've sworn, and I've done heaps of bad things: so *that's* out of the question. And I can't be a *found* sheep, because I don't love the Good Shepherd—I never think about Him at all; so I suppose I'm a *lost* sheep. That's a very bad thing to be, isn't it?'

'Yes, very bad! if you are always a lost sheep,' said the child; 'but if you are one of the lost sheep, then *Jesus came to seek you and to save you.*'

'Didn't He come to seek and save the old mother?' asked Jinx.

'Not if she's one of the ninety and nine,' said Rosalie. 'It says, "The Son of man is come to seek and to save that which was *lost*"; so if she isn't lost, it doesn't mean her.'

The woman looked very uncomfortable when Rosalie said this; she did not like to think that Jesus had not come to save her.

'Well, and suppose a fellow knows he's one of the lost sheep,' said Jinx, 'what has he got to do?'

'He must cry out to the Good Shepherd, and tell Him he's lost, and ask the Good Shepherd to find him.'

'Well, but first of all, I suppose,' said Jinx, 'he must make himself a *bit ready* to go to the Good Shepherd—leave off a few of his bad ways, and make himself decent a bit.'

'Oh no!' said Rosalie; 'he'd never get back to the fold that way. First of all, he must tell the Shepherd he's lost; and then the Shepherd, who has been seeking him a long, long time, will find him at once, and carry him on His shoulders home: and then the Good Shepherd will help him to do all the rest.'

'Well, I'll think about what you've said,' Jinx replied; 'thank you, little 'un.'

John Thomas here pulled up, saying it was two o'clock, and time they had dinner. So the caravans were drawn up by the roadside, and the woman took the dinner from the oven, and Jinx was sent to the next caravan with Lord Fatimore's dinner, and Rosalie, offering to help, was sent after him with the same gentleman's pipe and tobacco.

She found Lord Fatimore sitting in state in his own caravan. He was an immensely fat man, or rather an enormously overgrown boy, very swollen, and imbecile in appearance. He was lounging in an easy chair, looking the picture of indolence. He brightened up a little as he saw his dinner arriving—it was the great event of his day.

When Rosalie returned to the caravan the woman was alone, stroking Skirrywinks, who was lying on her knee, but looking as if her thoughts were far away.

'Child,' she said to Rosalie, 'I'm not one of the ninety and nine; I *do* need repentance; I'm one of the lost sheep.'

'I'm so glad,' said Rosalie, 'because then the Good Shepherd is seeking you: won't you ask Him to find you?'

Before she could answer John Thomas and Jinx came in for their dinner, and they all insisted on Rosalie joining them.

After dinner John Thomas sat in the caravan

and smoked, and Jinx drove, and Rosalie sat still thinking. She was so tired and worn out, that after a little time the picture on the wall, John Thomas, the woman, Skirrywinks, Tozer, and Spanco faded from her sight, and she fell fast asleep.

CHAPTER 20

MOTHER MANIKIN'S CHAIRS

WHEN Rosalie awoke it was almost dark. The woman was lighting the little oil-lamp, and filling the kettle from a large can of water, which stood in the corner of the caravan.

'Where are we?' said the child, in a sleepy voice.

'Close on Pendleton, little 'un,' answered Jinx; 'get up and see the lights in the distance.'

'Oh dear, and it's nearly dark!' said Rosalie.

'Never mind, my dear; we're just there,' said John Thomas. He did not know that she had five more miles to walk.

The wheels of the caravan rumbled on, and in about a quarter of an hour they came into the streets of the town. It was quite dark now, and the lamps were all lighted, and the men were going home from work.

Then they arrived at the field where the fair was held; the very field where the old man had given Rosalie the picture. Not many caravans had arrived, for John Thomas had come in good time.

Now Rosalie must leave her kind friends, which she did with many grateful thanks. Before she said good-bye she whispered a few words in the woman's ear.

'Yes, child; this very night I will,' answered the woman as she gave Rosalie a warm, loving kiss on her forehead.

Then the little girl went down the caravan steps, and turned into the neighbouring street. The Good Shepherd who had helped her so wonderfully as far as this would never leave her now. This was her one comfort. Yet she could not help feeling very lonely as she went down the street, and peeped in at the windows as she passed by. In nearly every house a bright fire was burning, and tea was ready on the table: in some, a happy family party was just sitting down to their evening meal: in all, there was an air of comfort and rest.

Rosalie, little, motherless Rosalie, was out in the cold, muddy, damp street alone, out in the darkness and the rain, and five miles from her aunt Lucy's house! How could she ever walk so far, that cold dark night? She trembled as she thought of going alone down those lonely country roads, without a light, without a friend to take care of her. Yet she would be still more afraid to wander about the streets of this great town, where she was sure there was so much wickedness and sin.

Even now there were very few people passing down the street, and Rosalie began to feel very much afraid of being out alone. She must find some one at once to show her the way to Melton.

The child was passing a small neat row of houses built close on the street. Most of them were shut up for the night, but through the cracks of the shutters Rosalie could see the bright light within.

The last house in the row was not yet shut up, and as Rosalie came near to it she saw a childish figure come out of the door, and go up to the shutters to close them. The fastener of the shutters had caught in the hook on the wall, and the little thing was too short to unloose it. She was standing on tip-toe, trying to undo it, when Rosalie came up.

'Let me help you,' she said, running up and unfastening the shutter.

'I'm extremely obliged to you,' said a voice behind her which made Rosalie start.

It was no child's voice; it was a voice she knew well, a voice she had often longed to hear. It was little Mother Manikin's voice!

With one glad cry of joy, Rosalie flung herself into the little woman's arms.

Mother Manikin drew back at first; it was dark, and she could not see Rosalie's face, but when the child said, in a tone of distress, 'Mother Manikin, dear Mother Manikin, don't you know me? I'm little Rosalie Joyce,' the dear little old woman was full of love and sympathy in a moment.

She dragged Rosalie indoors into a warm little kitchen at the back of the house, where the table was spread for tea, and a kettle was singing cheerily on the fire; and she sat on a stool beside her, with both her little hands grasping Rosalie's.

'And now, child,' she said, 'how ever did you find me out?'

'I didn't find you out, Mother Manikin,' said Rosalie; 'you found me out.'

'What do you mean, child?' said the old woman.

'Why, dear Mother Manikin, I didn't know you were here. I didn't know who it was till I had finished unfastening the shutter!'

'Bless me, child, then, what makes you out at

this time of night? Has your caravan just arrived at the fair?'

'No, dear Mother Manikin, I've not come to the fair. I'm quite alone, and I have five miles farther to walk.'

'Tell me all about it, child,' said Mother Manikin.

Rosalie told her all—told her how and where her mother died; told her about the lodging-house, and the woman of the house; told her about her father's marriage and death; told her of her aunt Lucy, and the letter and the locket; told her everything, as she would have told her own mother. For Mother Manikin had a motherly heart, and Rosalie knew it; and the tired child felt a wonderful sense of comfort and rest, in pouring out her sorrows into those sympathizing ears.

In the middle of Rosalie's story the little woman jumped up, saying hurriedly:

'Wait a minute, child; here's a strange kitten got in.'

She was just going to drive out the little black stranger, which was mewing loudly under the table, when the child stopped her.

'Please, dear Mother Manikin, that's my little kit; she has come with me all the way, and she's very hungry, that's why she makes such a noise.'

In another minute, a saucer of milk was placed on the rug before the fire, and the poor little kitten had enough and to spare.

Rosalie was very grateful to Mother Manikin, and very glad to be with her; but just as she was finishing her story the large eight-day clock in the

corner of the kitchen struck seven, and Rosalie
started to her feet.

'Mother Manikin,' she said, 'I must be off, I've
five miles farther to walk.'

'Stuff and nonsense, child!' said the old woman;
'do you think I'm going to let you go to-night?
Not a bit of it, I can tell you; old age must have its
liberties, my dear, and I'm not going to allow it.'

'Oh, Mother Manikin,' said Rosalie; 'what do
you mean?'

'What do I mean, child? Why, that you're to
sleep here to-night, and then go, all rested and
refreshed, to your aunt's to-morrow. That's what
I mean. Why, I have ever such a nice little house
here, bless you,' said the little woman; 'just you
come and look.'

She took Rosalie upstairs, and showed her the
neatest little bedroom in the front of the house, and
another room over the kitchen which Mother
Manikin called her greenhouse; for in it, arranged
on boxes near the window, were all manner of
flowerpots, containing all manner of flowers, ferns,
and mosses.

'It's a nice, sunny room, my dear,' said Mother
Manikin, 'and it's my hobby, you see; and old
age must have its liberties, and these little bits of
plants are my hobby. I live here all alone, and
they're company, you see. And now come downstairs and see my little parlour.'

The parlour was in the front of the house, and it
was the shutters of this room which Mother Manikin
was closing as Rosalie came up. A bright lamp
hung from the ceiling of the room, and white

muslin curtains adorned the window; but what struck Rosalie most of all was that the parlour was full of chairs. There were rows and rows of chairs; indeed, the parlour was so full of them that Mother Manikin and Rosalie could hardly find a place to stand.

'What a number of chairs you have here, Mother Manikin!' said the child in amazement.

The old woman laughed at Rosalie's astonished face.

'Rosalie, child,' she said, 'do you remember how you talked to me that night—the night when we sat up in the caravan?'

Rosalie's eyes filled with tears at the thought of it.

'Yes, dear Mother Manikin,' she answered.

'Do you remember how I looked at your picture, and you told me all about it?'

'Yes, Mother Manikin,' said the child, 'I remember that.'

'And you remember a *question* that you asked me then, Rosalie, child? "Mother Manikin," you said, "has *He* found *you*?" And I thought about it a long time: and then I told you the truth. I said, "No, child, He hasn't found me." But if you asked me that question to-night, Rosalie, child, if you asked little Mother Manikin, "Do you think the Good Shepherd has found you *now*, Mother Manikin?" I should tell you, Rosalie, child, I should tell you that He went about to seek and save them which were lost, and that one day, when He was seeking, He found little Mother Manikin!

'Yes, my dear,' said the old woman, 'He found me. I cried out to Him that I was lost, and wanted finding, and He heard me, child: He heard me, and He carried me on His shoulders rejoicing!'

Little Rosalie could not help crying when she heard this, but they were tears of joy.

'I gave up the fairs, child; it didn't seem as if I could follow the Good Shepherd there; there was a lot of foolishness, and nonsense, and distraction! So I left them. I told them old age must have its liberties, and I brought away my savings, and a little sum of money I had of my own, and I took this little house. So that's how it is, child,' said the little old woman.

'But about the chairs?' said Rosalie.

'Yes, about the chairs,' repeated the old woman; 'I'm coming to that now. I was sitting one night thinking, my dear, over the kitchen fire: I was thinking about the Good Shepherd, and how He had died for me, just that I might be found and brought back to the fold. And I thought, child, when He had been so good to me, it was very bad of me to do nothing for Him in return, nothing to show Him I'm grateful, you see. I shook my fist, and I said to myself, you ought to be ashamed of yourself, Mother Manikin, you little idle, ungrateful old thing!

'Then, Rosalie, child, I began to think, What can I do? I'm so little, you see, and folks laugh at me, and run after me when I go out, and all things seemed closed on me. There seemed nothing for little Mother Manikin to do for the Good Shepherd. So I knelt down, child, and I asked Him. I said:

'"*O Good Shepherd, have You got any work for a*

woman that's only three feet high? Because I do love You, and want to do it."

'Well, Rosalie, child, it came quite quick, after that; Mr. Westerdale called, and said he:

'"Mother Manikin, I want to have a little Bible meeting for some of the people round here: the mothers who have little babies, and can't get to any place of worship, and a few more, who are often ill, and can't walk far. Do you know anybody in this row who would let me have a room for my class?"

'Well, child, I danced for joy; I really did, child; I danced like I hadn't danced since I left the Royal Show. So Mr. Westerdale, he says, "What's the matter, Mother Manikin?" He thought I'd gone clean off my head.

'"Why, Mr. Westerdale," I cried, "there's something I can do for the Good Shepherd, though I'm only three feet high!"

'So then he understood, child, and he finds the parlour very convenient, and the people come so nicely; and it's a happy night for me. That's what the chairs are for.

'Mr. Westerdale will be here in a minute, child; he always gets a cup of tea with me before the folks come. That's why I'm so late to-night; I always wait till he comes.'

She had no sooner said the words than a rap was heard at the door, and the little woman ran to open it for Mr. Westerdale. He was an old man, with a rosy, good-tempered face, and a kind and cheerful voice.

'Well, Mother Manikin,' he said, as he came

into the kitchen, 'a good cup of tea ready for me as usual! What a good, kind woman you are!'

'This is a little friend of mine, Mr. Westerdale,' said Mother Manikin, introducing Rosalie.

However, Rosalie needed no introduction. She shook hands with the old man, and then darted out of the room, and in another minute returned with her small bag, which she had left upstairs. Hastily unfastening it, she took from it her dear picture, the picture which had done so much for her and her mother and little Mother Manikin, and holding it up before the old man, she cried out:

'Please, sir, it's quite safe; I've kept it all this time, and, please, I do love it so!'

For Mr. Westerdale was Rosalie's old friend, who had come to see her in the fair, just a year ago. He did not remember her, but he remembered the picture; and when Rosalie told him where she had seen him, a recollection of the sick woman and her pretty child came back to his mind. As they sat over their comfortable little tea, and Rosalie told how that picture had been the messenger of mercy to her dying mother, the old man's face became brighter than ever.

After tea the people began to arrive. It was a pleasant sight to see how little Mother Manikin welcomed them, one by one, as they came in. They all seemed to know her well, and to love her, and trust her. She had many questions to ask them, and they had much to tell her. There was Teddy's cough to be inquired after, and grandfather's rheumatism, and the baby's chicken-pox. Mother Manikin must be told how Willie had got that situation he was trying for, how old Mrs. Joyce had got a letter from her daughter at last, how Mrs. Price's daughter had broken her leg, and Mrs. Price had told them to say how glad she would be if Mother Manikin could go in to see her for a few minutes sometimes.

Little Mother Manikin had 'a heart at leisure from itself, to soothe and sympathize.' Their troubles were her troubles, their joys her joys.

At last every one had arrived, and the chairs in the sitting-room were all filled. Then the clock struck eight, and they were all quite still as Mr. Westerdale gave out the hymn. When the hymn and the prayer were ended, Mr. Westerdale began to speak. Rosalie was sitting close to Mother Manikin, and she listened very attentively to all that her old friend said.

'Though your sins be as scarlet, they shall be as white as snow'; that was the text of the sermon.

'A long way from here, my friends,' said Mr. Westerdale, 'a long way from here, in the land of Palestine, is a beautiful mountain, the top of which is covered with the purest, whitest snow. One day, a very great many years ago, the Apostle John and two of his friends were lying on the mountain asleep, and when they awoke they saw a wonderful sight. They saw the Lord Jesus in His Glory, and His raiment was exceeding white—as white as snow.

'A few years later, God let this same Apostle John look into heaven; and there he saw everything the same colour, pure, unstained white. The Lord Jesus had His head and His hair as white as wool, as white as snow. He was sitting on a white throne, and all the vast multitude standing round the throne had white robes on—pure, spotless white, as white as snow.

'Nothing, my friends, that is not perfectly white can enter heaven, for pure, perfect white is heaven's colour.

'What does all this mean? It means that nothing can enter that holy heaven that is not perfectly pure, perfectly holy, perfectly free from sin.

'For there is another colour mentioned in my text, a colour which is just the opposite to white, *scarlet*—glaring scarlet. And this colour is used as a picture of that which is not pure, not holy, that on which God cannot look—I mean sin.

'Your sins are as scarlet, God says; and no scarlet can enter heaven; nothing is found within the gates of heaven but pure white, as white as snow. Nothing short of perfect holiness can admit you or me into heaven. When we stand before the gate, it will be no good our pleading, I'm almost white, I'm nearly white, I'm whiter than my neighbours: nothing but pure white, nay, white as snow, will avail us anything. One single scarlet spot is enough to shut the gates of heaven against us.

'This is a very solemn thought. For who in this room, which of you mothers, which of you young girls, can stand up and say, "There is no scarlet spot on me, I am free from sin? Heaven's gate would be opened to me, for I have never done anything wrong—I am quite white, as white as snow?"

'Which of you can say that? Which of you would dare to say it if you stood before the gate of Heaven to-night?

P

'"There is no hope, then," you say, "for me; heaven's gates are for ever closed against me. I have sinned over and over again. I am covered with scarlet spots, nay, I am altogether scarlet.

> '"Red like crimson, deep as scarlet,
>   Scarlet of the deepest dye,
>   Are the manifold transgressions,
>   Which upon my conscience lie!
>
> '"God alone can count their number!
>   God alone can look within;
>   Oh the sinfulness of sinning!
>   Oh the guilt of every sin!

'"There is no hope, not the least for me! Only spotless white can enter heaven; so I must be for ever shut out!"'

'Must you? Is there indeed no hope?

'Listen, oh listen again to the text, "Though your sins be as scarlet, they shall be as white as snow."

'Then there is a way of changing the scarlet into white; there is a way of making the deep glaring scarlet turn into pure white, as white as snow.

'Oh! what good news for us! What glad tidings of great joy!

'How is it done? How can you or I, who are so covered with scarlet stains of sin, be made as white as snow?

'My friends, *this* is the way. There is One, the Lord Jesus Christ, who has been punished instead of us, who has taken all our sins on Him, just as if they were His own sins, and has been punished

for them, as if He had really done them. The great
God who loved us so planned all this. And now
He can forgive us our sins, for the punishment is
over. He can not only forgive, but He can forget.
He can blot our sins out. He can make us clean
and white, as white as snow.

'This then is His offer to you to-night. "Come
now," He cries, "only accept My offer." Take the
Lord Jesus Christ as your Saviour; only ask Him
to wash you in His blood; only see, by faith, that
He died in your place, instead of you, and your
sins—your scarlet sins—shall be made as white as
snow. This very night, before you lie down to
sleep, you may be made so white, that heaven's
gate, when you stand before it, will be thrown wide
open to you; so white, that you will be fit to stand
among that great multitude which no man can
number who have washed their robes and made
them white in the blood of the Lamb.

'My dear friends, will you accept God's offer?
Will you come to the Lord Jesus to be made white?
Will you plead this promise, the promise in my
text? Will you, before you lie down to sleep, say:

'"O Lord, my sins are indeed as scarlet, make
them, in the blood of Christ, as white as snow"?

'Will you, I ask you again, accept God's offer?
Yes, or No?'

CHAPTER 21

IN SIGHT OF HOME

WHEN the little service was over Mr. Westerdale, Mother Manikin, and Rosalie sat together over the fire talking. The old man was much encouraged by all that he heard from the child. He had sometimes wondered whether his visits to the fair had done the slightest good to any one, and now that he heard how God had so largely blessed this one picture, he felt strengthened and cheered to make further efforts for the benefit of the poor travellers, whose souls so few care for. Next Sunday would be the Sunday for him to visit the shows, he said, and he should go there this year with more hope and more faith.

When Rosalie heard this she begged him to have a little conversation with the woman with whom she had travelled. She told him to look out for the show over the door of which was written, 'Lord Fatimore and other Pleasing Varieties,' for there, she felt sure, he would find a work to do. And she did not forget to ask him, when he went there, to remember to inquire for Jinx, and to speak to him also.

When Mr. Westerdale had said good-night and was gone away, Mother Manikin insisted on Rosalie's going at once to bed, for the child was very weary with her long and tiring day.

She slept very soundly, and in the morning

awoke to find Mother Manikin standing beside her
with a cup of tea in her hands.

'Come, child,' she said, 'drink this before you
get up.'

'O dear Mother Manikin,' said Rosalie, starting
up, 'how good you are to me!'

'Bless you, child,' said the dear little old woman,
'I only wish you could stay with me altogether;
now mind me, child, if you find when you get to
Melton that it isn't convenient for you to stay at
your aunt's, just you come back to me. Dear me,
how comfortable you and me might be together!
I'm lonesome at times here, and want a bit of
company; and my little bit of money is enough for
both of us. So mind you, child,' repeated Mother
Manikin, shaking her little fist at Rosalie, 'if you
don't find all quite straight at Melton, if you think
it puts them out at all to take you in, you come to
me. Now I've said it, and when I've said it I mean
it; old age must have its liberties, and I must be
obeyed.'

'Dear Mother Manikin!' said Rosalie, putting
her arms round the little old woman's neck, 'I
can never, never, never say thank you often
enough.'

After breakfast Rosalie started on her journey,
with the little black kit in its usual place in her
arms. Mother Manikin insisted on wrapping up a
little parcel, containing lunch, for the child to eat
on her way. And as she stood on the door-step to
see her off she called out after her:

'Now, child, if all isn't quite straight, come back
here to-night; I shall be looking out for you.'

So Rosalie started on her journey. On her way she passed the field where the fair was to be held. What recollections it brought to her mind of the year before, when she had arrived there in the caravan with her sick mother!

Not many shows had reached the place, for it was yet three days before the fair would be held. But in one corner of the field Rosalie discovered the bright yellow caravans of the show of 'Lord Fatimore and other Pleasing Varieties.' She could not pass by without going for a moment to the caravan to thank Old Mother, and John Thomas, and Jinx for their kindness to her the day before.

Mother was having a great wash of all John Thomas's clothes, and Lord Fatimore's, and Jinx's, and her own. She was standing at the door of the caravan washing, and Jinx was busily engaged hanging out the clothes on a line which had been stretched between the two caravans.

'Halloa, young 'un!' said he, as Rosalie came up, 'and where have you sprung from?'

Rosalie told him that she had spent the night with a friend who lived in the town, and was going to continue her journey.

'Young 'un,' said Jinx, 'I haven't forgot what you told me about that there picture. I like my picture a deal more than I did afore.'

Then Rosalie went up to the woman, who did not see her till she was close to the caravan steps. She was hard at work at her washing, with Skirry-winks sitting on her shoulder, and Spanco, the pigeon, on her head. Rosalie could not be quite

sure, but she fancied there were tears in her eyes
as she bent over her washing.

'Oh, it's you!' she said to Rosalie. 'I am glad to
see you again; I was thinking about you just then.'

'Were you?' said the child; 'what were you
thinking?'

'I was thinking over what we talked about
yesterday—about the lost sheep.'

'Did you remember last night to ask the Good
Shepherd to find you?' said Rosalie.

'Oh, yes!' said the woman; 'I didn't forget;
but instead of the Good Shepherd finding me, I
think I'm farther away from the fold than ever;
leastways I never knew I was so bad before.'

'Then the Good Shepherd is going to find you,'
said Rosalie; 'He only waits until we know we are
lost, and then He is ready to find us at once.'

'Oh! I do hope so,' said the woman, earnestly;
'you'll think of me sometimes, won't you?'

'Yes, I'll never forget you,' said the child.

'Will you come in and rest a bit?'

'No, thank you, ma'am,' said Rosalie; 'I must
go now; I have some way farther to walk; but I
wanted to say good-bye to you, and to thank you
for being so kind to me yesterday.'

'Bless you!' said the woman, heartily; 'it was
nothing to speak of. Good-bye, child, and mind
you think of me sometimes.'

Rosalie left the fair-field and turned on to the
Melton Road. A strange feeling came over her
then. She was within five miles of her aunt Lucy,
and was really going to her at last! How she had
longed to see the dear face she had gazed at so often

in the locket! How she had yearned to deliver her mother's letter, and to see her aunt Lucy reading it! How often—how very often—all this had been in her mind by day, and had mingled with her dreams at night!

Yet now—now that she was really on the road which led up to her aunt Lucy's door—Rosalie's heart failed her. She looked down at her little frock, and saw how very old and faded it was. She took off her hat, and the piece of black ribbon which Toby had given her had never before seemed so rusty and brown.

What a shabby little girl her aunt Lucy would see coming in at the garden-gate! Her thoughts travelled back to the little girl whom she had seen in that garden a year ago, her aunt Lucy's own little girl. How differently she was dressed! How unlike in every way she was to Rosalie! What if her aunt Lucy was vexed with her for coming? She had often been troubled by Rosalie's father; was it likely she would welcome his child?

Sometimes Rosalie felt inclined to turn back and go to old Mother Manikin. But she remembered how her mother had said:

'If ever you can, dear, you must go to your aunt Lucy, and give her that letter.'

Whatever it cost her, Rosalie determined she would go. But she grew more and more shy as she drew nearer the village, and walked far more slowly than she had done when she first left the town.

At last the village of Melton came in sight. It was a fine spring morning, and the sunlight was falling softly on the cottages and farm-houses and the beautiful green trees and hedges.

Rosalie rested a little on a stile before she went farther, and the little black kit basked in the sunshine. The field close by was full of sheep, and the child sat and watched them. It was a very pretty field; there were groups of trees, under the shadow of which the sheep could lie and rest; and there was a quiet stream trickling through the midst of the field, from which the sheep could drink the cool, refreshing water.

As Rosalie watched the sheep in their happy, quiet field, a verse of the psalm which Popsey's old grandfather had read came into her mind.

'He maketh me to lie down in green pastures; He leadeth me beside the still waters.'

What if the Good Shepherd were about to take her, His poor little motherless lamb, to a green pasture, a quiet restful home, where she might be taught more of the Good Shepherd's love? How Rosalie prayed that it might indeed be so! And then she summoned courage and went on.

It was about twelve o'clock when she reached Melton. The country people were most of them having their dinner, and few people were in the village street. With a beating heart the child pressed on.

Soon she came in sight of the little cottage, before which the caravan had stood when she and her mother were there a year ago. There was the cottage with its thatched roof, looking just as comfortable as it had done then; there was the garden just the same as before with the same kind of flowers growing in it; there were the cabbage-roses, the southernwood, the rosemary, the sweet-briar, and the lavender. The wind was blowing softly over them, and wafting their sweet fragrance to Rosalie just as it had done a year ago.

And there was Rosalie, standing peeping through the gate, just as she had done then. It seemed to Rosalie like a dream which she had dreamt before. Only a year—only a year ago!

Yet one was absent; her mother was no more there; she was gone; and little Rosalie was alone by the gate!

As she looked through the bars, tears came in her eyes and fell on her little dusty frock. But she wiped them away, and went on through the village street.

At length she arrived at the large house close to the church which her mother had longed so much to see. With a trembling hand she opened the iron gate and walked up the broad gravel path.

There was a large knocker in the middle of the door, and a bell on one side of it. Rosalie did not know whether to knock or to ring, so she stood still for a few minutes without doing either, hoping that someone would see her from the window and come to ask what she wanted.

As the minutes passed by and no one came, Rosalie ventured, very gently and timidly, to rap with the knocker, but no one inside the house heard the sound of the child's knocking. So she gathered courage and pulled the bell, which rang so loudly that it made her tremble more than ever.

Then she heard a rustling in the hall and the

sound of a quick footstep, and the door was opened. A girl about eighteen years of age stood before her, dressed in a pretty print dress and very white apron, with a neat round cap on her head. Rosalie was trembling so much now that she cast her eyes on the ground and did not speak.

'What do you want, dear?' said the girl, kindly, stooping down to Rosalie as she spoke.

'If you please,' said Rosalie, 'is Mrs. Leslie in? I have a letter that I want very much to give her.'

'No, dear; she's not in just now,' said the girl; 'will you leave the letter with me?'

'Oh, please,' said Rosalie, timidly, 'I would very much like to give it to her myself, if you will be so kind as to let me wait till she comes.'

'Yes, she won't be very long,' said the girl. 'Would you like to sit in the summer-house till she comes? It's very pleasant there.'

'Oh, thank you,' said the child, gratefully; 'I should like it very much indeed.'

'I'll show you where it is,' said the girl; 'it's behind these trees.'

As Rosalie was walking to the summer-house she ventured for the first time to look into the girl's face. The voice had seemed familiar to her; but when she saw the face, the large brown eyes, the dark hair, and the rosy cheeks, she felt sure that she had met with an old friend.

'Oh, please,' she said, stopping suddenly short in the path, 'please aren't you Britannia?'

'How do you know anything about Britannia?' she inquired, hurriedly.

'I didn't mean to say Britannia,' said Rosalie.

'I know you don't ever want to be called *that* again; but, please, you are Jessie, are you not?'

'Yes, dear,' said the girl; 'my name is Jessie; but how do you know me?'

'Please,' said Rosalie, 'don't you remember me? And how we talked in the caravan that windy night, when my mummy was so ill?'

'Oh, Rosalie!' said Jessie, 'is it you? Why, to think I never knew you! Why, I shouldn't ever have been here if it hadn't been for you and your mother! Oh, I am glad to see you again! Where are you going to, dear? Is your caravan at Pendleton fair?'

'No, Jessie,' said Rosalie; 'I don't live in a caravan now; and I've walked here to give a letter from my mother to Mrs. Leslie.'

'Then your mother got better after all,' said Jessie; 'I am so glad! she was so very ill that night!'

'Oh, no! no! no!' said Rosalie, with a flood of tears; 'no! she didn't get better; she wrote that letter a long time ago.'

'Poor little Rosalie!' said Jessie, putting her arms round her, and shedding tears also; 'I am so very, very sorry!'

'Please, Jessie,' said Rosalie, through her tears, 'did you remember to give Mrs. Leslie my mummy's message?'

'Yes, dear, that I did. Do you think I would forget anything she asked me? Why, I should never have been here if it hadn't been for her.'

'Can you remember what you said to Mrs. Leslie, Jessie?'

'Yes, dear. It was the first time she came to our house after I came back. I told her all about what I had done, and where I had been. And then I told her how I had met with a woman who used to know her many years ago, but who hadn't seen her for a long, long time, and that this woman had sent her a message. So she asked me who this woman was, and what the message was which she had sent her. I told her that the woman's name was Norah, but I didn't know her other name, and that Norah sent her respects and her love, and I was to say that she had not very long to live, but that the Good Shepherd had sought her and found her, and that she was not afraid to die. Then, Rosalie, she cried when I told her that, and went away. But she came again about half an hour after that, and asked me ever so many questions about your mother, and I told her all I could. I told her how ill she was, and how she liked the hymn, and all about you, and how good you were to your mother. And then I told her how beautifully your mother talked to me about the Good Shepherd, and how she begged me to ask the Good Shepherd to find me, and how I had done as she begged me, and I hoped that He was carrying me home on His shoulder. And I told her, dear, how kind you both were to me, and how you gave me that money, and made me promise to know which road the caravan was on, and which fair it was going to. She asked many questions about that, and wanted to know if I could tell her what town would be the next you would stop at after the one you were going to when I met you; but I couldn't. Now I must go in, dear, and get dinner ready; but I'll tell my mistress as soon as she comes.'

So Rosalie sat down in the arbour to wait. But she could hardly sit still a minute, she felt so excited and restless.

Only now and again she lifted up her heart in prayer to the Good Shepherd, asking Him to make her aunt love her and help her.

CHAPTER 22

THE LOST LAMB FOUND

THE time that Rosalie waited in the arbour seemed very, very long to her. Every minute was like an hour, and at the least sound she started from her seat, and looked down the gravel path. But it was only a bird, or a falling leaf, or some other trifling sound, which Rosalie's anxious ears had exaggerated.

At last, when the sound she had been listening for so long did really come, when footsteps were heard on the gravel path coming towards the arbour, Rosalie sat still until they drew close, for in a moment all the fears she had by the way returned on her.

They were very quick and eager footsteps which Rosalie heard, and in another moment, almost before she knew that her aunt Lucy had entered the arbour, she found herself locked in her arms.

'Oh, my little Rosalie,' said she, with a glad cry; 'have I found you at last?'

For Jessie had told Mrs. Leslie that it was Norah's child who was waiting to speak to her in the arbour.

Rosalie could not speak. For a long time after that she was too full of feeling for any words. And her aunt Lucy could only say, over and over again, 'My little Rosalie, have I found you at last?' It seemed to Rosalie more like what the Good Shepherd said of His lost sheep than anything she had ever heard before.

'Have you been looking for me, dear aunt Lucy?' she said at last.

'Yes, darling, indeed I have!' said her aunt. 'Ever since Jessie came back I have been trying to find out where you were. I wanted so much to see your mother; but before I arrived at the place she was dead. I saw her grave, Rosalie, darling; I heard about her dying in the fair; and my husband found out where she was buried, and we went and stood by her grave. And ever since then, dear child, I have been looking for you; but I had lost all clue to you, and was almost giving it up in despair. But I've found you now, darling, and I am so very thankful.'

Then Rosalie opened her bag and took out the precious letter. How her aunt Lucy's hand trembled as she opened it! It was like getting a letter from another world! And then she began to read, but her eyes were so full of tears that she could hardly see the words.

'MY OWN DARLING SISTER,

'I am writing this letter with the faint hope that Rosalie may one day give it to you. It ought not to be a faint hope, because I have turned it so often into a prayer. Oh, how many times have I thought of you since last we met, how often in my dreams you have come to me and spoken to me!

'I am too ill and too weak to write much, but I want to tell you that your many prayers for me have been answered at last. The lost sheep has been found, and has been carried back to the fold. I think I am the greatest sinner that ever lived, and yet I believe my sins are washed away in the blood of Jesus.

'I would write more, but am too exhausted. But I want to ask you (if it is possible for you to do so) to save my sweet Rosalie from her mother's fate. She is such a dear child. I know you would love her—and I am so very unhappy about leaving her among all these temptations.

'I know I do not deserve any favour from you, and you cannot think what pain it gives me to think how often you have been asked for money in my name! That has been one of the greatest trials of my unhappy life.

'But if you can save my little Rosalie, oh, dear sister, I think even in heaven I shall know it, and be more glad. I would ask you to do it, not for my sake, for I deserve nothing but shame and disgrace, but for the sake of Him who has said, "Whoso shall receive one such little child in My name receiveth Me."

'Your Loving Sister,
'NORAH.'

'When did your dear mother write the letter, Rosalie?' aunt Lucy asked, as soon as she could speak after she had finished reading it.

Rosalie told her that it was written only a few days before her mother died. And then she put her hand inside her dress, and brought out the locket, which she laid in Mrs. Leslie's hand.

'Do you remember *that*, aunt Lucy?' she said.

'Yes, darling, I do,' said her aunt; 'I gave that to your mother years ago, before she left home; I remember I saved up my money a very long time that I might buy it.'

'My mother did love that locket so much,' said the child. 'She said she had promised you she would keep it as long as she lived; and I was to tell you she had kept her promise, and had hidden it away, lest any one should take it from her. I have tried so hard to keep it safe since she died; but we

Q

have been in a big lodging-house all the winter, and I was so afraid it would be found and taken from me.'

'Where is your father now, Rosalie?' asked her aunt, anxiously.

'He's dead,' said the child; 'he has been dead more than a week.' And she told of the accident and the death in the hospital.

'Then you are my little girl now, Rosalie,' said her aunt Lucy, 'my own little girl, and no one can take you from me.'

'Oh, dear aunt Lucy, may I really stay?'

'Why, Rosalie darling, I have been looking for you everywhere, and my only fear was that your father would not want to part with you. But now before we talk any more, you must come in and see your uncle; he is very anxious to see you.'

Rosalie felt rather afraid again when her aunt said this. But she rose up to follow her into the house. And then she remembered the little kitten, which she covered with her shawl, and which was lying fast asleep under it in a corner of the arbour.

'Please, aunt Lucy,' said Rosalie, timidly, 'is there a bird?'

'Where, dear?' said Mrs. Leslie, looking round her. 'I don't see one.'

'No, not here in the garden,' explained Rosalie; 'I mean in your house.'

'No, there's no bird, dear child; what made you think there was one?'

'Oh, I'm so glad, so very, very glad!' said Rosalie, with tears in her eyes—'then may I bring her?'

'Bring who, Rosalie dear? I don't understand.'

'Oh, aunt Lucy,' said the child, 'don't be angry; I have a little kit here, under my shawl. She's the dearest little kit, and we love each other so much, and if she had to go away from me I think she would die. She loved me when no one else in the lodging-house did, except Betsey Ann; and if only she may come I'll never let her go in any of the best rooms, and I won't let her be any trouble.' When she had said this she lifted up the shawl, and brought out the black kitten, and looked up beseechingly into her aunt's face.

'What a dear little kitten!' said her aunt. 'May will be pleased with it; she is so fond of kittens; and only the other day I promised her I would get one. Bring her in, and she shall have some milk.'

A great load was lifted off little Rosalie's heart when Mrs. Leslie said this, for it would have been a very great trial to her to part from her little friend.

Rosalie's uncle received her very kindly, and said, with a pleasant smile, that he was glad the little prairie flower had been found at last, and was to blossom in his garden. Then she went upstairs with her aunt Lucy to get ready for dinner. She thought she had never seen such a beautiful room as Mrs. Leslie's bedroom. The windows looked out over the fields and trees to the blue hills beyond.

Then her aunt went to a wardrobe which stood at one end of the room, and brought out a parcel, which she opened, and inside Rosalie saw a beautiful little black dress, very neatly and prettily made.

'This is a dress which came home last night for my little May,' said her aunt; 'but I think it will fit you, dear; will you try it on?'

'Oh, aunt Lucy!' said Rosalie, 'what a beautiful frock! But won't May want it?'

'No; May is from home,' said Mrs. Leslie; 'she is staying with your uncle Gerald; there will be plenty of time to have another made for her before she returns.'

Rosalie hardly knew herself in the new dress, and felt very shy at first; but it fitted her exactly, and her aunt Lucy was very pleased indeed.

Then Mrs. Leslie brought a black ribbon, and tied the precious locket round the little girl's neck; there was no longer any need to hide it.

After this they went downstairs, and Rosalie had a place given her at dinner between her uncle and aunt. Jessie looked very much astonished when she was told to put another knife and fork and plate on the table for Rosalie; but her mistress, seeing her surprised face, called her into another room, and in a few words told her who the little girl was, at the same time begging her, for Rosalie's sake, not to mention to any one in the village where and how she had seen the child before. This Jessie most willingly promised. 'There is nothing I would not do for Rosalie's sake,' she said, 'for I should never have been here had it not been for Rosalie and her mother.'

That afternoon the child sat on a stool at her aunt Lucy's feet, and they had a long talk, which little Rosalie enjoyed more than words can tell.

She gave her aunt a little history of her life, going back as far as she could remember. Oh, how eagerly Mrs. Leslie listened to anything about her poor sister! How many questions she asked, and how many tears she shed!

When Rosalie had finished, her aunt told her once more how glad and thankful she was to have her there, and more especially as she felt sure that her little Rosalie loved the Good Shepherd, and tried to please Him, and therefore would never, never do any harm to her own little May, but would rather help her in all that was right.

The child slipped her hand in that of her aunt Lucy when she said this, with a very loving and assuring smile. 'So now, Rosalie dear, you must look on me as your mother,' said Mrs. Leslie; 'you must tell me all your troubles, and ask me for anything you want, just as you would have asked your own dear mother.'

'Please, aunt Lucy,' said Rosalie, gratefully, 'I think the pasture is very green indeed.'

'What do you mean, my dear child?'

'I mean, aunt Lucy, I have been very lonely and often very miserable lately; but the Good Shepherd has brought me at last to a very green pasture; don't you think He has?'

But Mrs. Leslie could only answer the little girl by taking her in her arms and kissing her.

That night, when Rosalie went upstairs to bed, Jessie came into her room to bring her some hot water.

'Oh, Jessie,' said Rosalie, 'how are Maggie and the baby?'

'To think you remembered about them!' said Jessie. 'They are quite well. Oh, you must see them soon!'

'Then they were all right when you got home,' said the child, 'were they, Jessie?'

'Oh, yes, God be thanked!' said Jessie; 'I didn't deserve it. Oh, how often I thought of those children when I lay awake those miserable nights in the circus. They had cried themselves to sleep, poor little things; when my mother came back she found them lying asleep on the floor.'

'Wasn't she very much frightened?' asked Rosalie.

'Yes, that she was,' said Jessie, with tears in her eyes; 'she was so ill when I came home that I thought she would die, and that I had killed her. She had hardly slept a wink since I went away, and she was as thin as a ghost. I hardly should have known her anywhere else.'

'But what did she say when you came back?'

'Oh! she wasn't angry a bit,' said Jessie; 'only she cried so, and was so glad to have me back that it seemed almost worse to bear than if she had scolded. And then quite quickly she began to get better; but if I hadn't come then I believe she would have died.'

'Is she quite well now?' asked the child.

'Yes; quite strong and well again, and as bright as ever. She was so glad when Mrs. Leslie said I might come here and be her housemaid. My mother says it's a grand thing to lie down to sleep at night feeling that her children are all safe; and she can never thank God enough for all He has done for me. I told her of you and your mother, and she prays for you every day, my mother does, that God may reward and bless you.'

The next morning, when Rosalie opened her eyes, she could not at first remember where she was. She had been dreaming she was in the dismal lodging-house, and that Betsey Ann was touching her hand, and waking her for their ten minutes' reading.

When she looked up, it was only her little black kitten which was feeling strange in its new home, and had crept up to her, and was licking her arm.

'Poor little kit!' said Rosalie, as she stroked it gently; 'you don't know where you are.' The kitten purred contentedly when its little mistress comforted it, and the child was at leisure to look round the room.

It was her cousin May's little room; and her aunt Lucy had said she might sleep there until another room just like it was made ready for her. Rosalie was lying in a small and very pretty iron bedstead with white muslin hangings. She peeped out of her little nest into the room beyond.

Through the window she could see the fields and the trees and the blue hills, just as she had done from her aunt Lucy's windows. The furniture of the room was very neat and pretty, and Rosalie looked at it with admiring eyes. Over the washhand-stand, and over the chest of drawers, were hung beautiful illuminated texts, and Rosalie read them one by one as she lay in bed. There was also a little book-case full of May's books, and a little wardrobe for May's clothes. How much Rosalie wondered what her cousin was like, and how she wished the time would arrive for her to come home!

Then the little girl jumped out of bed, and went to the window to look out. The garden beneath her looked very lovely in the bright morning sunshine; the roses and geraniums and jessamine were just in their glory, and underneath the trees she could see patches of lovely ferns and mosses. How she wished her mother could have been there to see them also! she had always loved flowers so much.

Rosalie dressed herself, and went out into the garden. How sweet and peaceful everything seemed! She went to the gate—that gate which she had looked through a year before—and gazed out into the blue distance. As she was doing so, she heard the sound of wheels, and three or four caravans bound for Pendleton fair went slowly down the road.

What a rush of feeling came over the child as she looked at them! Oh, how kind the Good Shepherd had been to her! Here she was, safe and sheltered in this quiet, happy home; and she would never, never have to go to a fair or a theatre again. Rosalie looked up at the blue sky above, and said from the bottom of her heart:

'O Good Shepherd, I do thank Thee very much for bringing me to the green pasture. Oh help me to love Thee and please Thee more than ever. Amen.'

CHAPTER 23

THE GREEN PASTURE

THAT morning, after breakfast, Mrs. Leslie took
Rosalie with her in the pony carriage to Pendleton.
She wanted to buy the furniture for the child's
little bedroom.

Rosalie enjoyed the drive very much indeed, and
was charmed and delighted with all the purchases
which her aunt made.

When they were finished, Rosalie said, 'Aunt
Lucy, do you think we should have time to call for
a minute on old Mother Manikin? She will want
so much to hear whether I got safely to Melton.'

Mrs. Leslie willingly consented; she had felt very
grateful to the little old woman for all her kindness
to her poor sister and her little niece, and she was
glad of an opportunity of thanking her for it.

They found Mother Manikin very poorly, but
very pleased indeed to see Rosalie. She had been
taken ill in the night, she said, quite suddenly. It
was something the matter with her heart. In the
morning she had asked one of the neighbours to
go for the doctor, and he had said it was not right
for her to be in the house alone.

'What am I to do, ma'am?' said Mother Manikin;
'here's the doctor says I must have a girl; but I
can't bear all these new-fangled creatures, with
their flounces, and their airs, and their manners.
Old age must have its liberties; and I can't put

up with them. No, I can't abide them,' she said, shaking her little fist. 'You couldn't tell me of a girl, could you, ma'am? I can't give very high wages, but she should have a comfortable home.'

'Oh! aunt Lucy,' cried Rosalie, springing from her seat, 'what do you think of Betsey Ann; would she do?'

'Who's Betsey Ann, child?' inquired Mother Manikin.

Rosalie told Betsey Ann's sad story; how she had been born in an institution; how she had never had any one to love her, but how she had been scolded and found fault with from morning till night.

Mother Manikin could hardly keep from crying as the story went on.

'She shall come at once,' said she, decidedly, as soon as Rosalie had finished; 'tell me where she lives, and I'll get Mr. Westerdale to write to her at once.'

'Oh, but she can't read,' said Rosalie, in a very distressed voice; 'and her mistress would never let her have the letter. What are we to do?'

When Mother Manikin heard where Betsey Ann lived, she said there would be no difficulty at all about it; Mr. Westerdale knew the Scripture reader there; she had often heard him speak of him; and he would be able to go to the house and make it all right.

So Rosalie felt very comforted about poor Betsey Ann.

Rosalie's first week in the green pasture passed by very happily. She walked and read and talked with her aunt Lucy, and went with her to see the poor people in the village, and grew to love her more day by day, and was more and more thankful to the Good Shepherd for the green pasture to which He had brought her.

After a week May came home. Such a bright little creature she was; Rosalie loved her as soon as she saw her. But it was no strange face to Rosalie; it was a face she had often gazed at and often studied, for little May was the image of the girl in the locket; it might have been her own picture, she was so like what her mother was at her age.

May and Rosalie were the best friends at once, and from that time had everything in common. They did their lessons together, they walked together, and they played together, and were never known to quarrel or to disagree.

Some little time after May's return, the two children went in the pony carriage to Pendleton. They had two important things to do there. One was to buy a present for Popsey, the little girl with the pitcher of milk; and the other was to call on Mother Manikin to see if Betsey Ann had arrived.

The two children had each had a half-sovereign given them by Mr. Leslie; and Rosalie wished to spend hers in something very nice for little Popsey. But the difficulty was to choose what it should be. All the way to Pendleton May was proposing different things—a book, a work-box, a writing-case; but at the mention of all of these Rosalie shook her head. 'Popsey was too small for any of these,' she said; 'she could not read, nor sew, nor write.' So then May proposed a doll, and Rosalie thought that it was a very good idea.

Palmer, the old coachman, was asked to drive to a toy-shop; and then, after a long consultation, and an immense comparison of wax dolls, composition dolls, china dolls, rag dolls, and wooden dolls, a beautiful china doll very splendidly dressed was chosen, and laid aside for Rosalie.

As she still had some money left, she also chose a very pretty spectacle-case for Popsey's grandfather, and a beautiful little milk-jug for the kind old grandmother. The milk-jug was a white one, and the handle was formed by a cat which was supposed to be climbing up the side of the jug and peeping into the milk. Rosalie was delighted with this, and fixed on it at once. For she had not forgotten the little pitcher of milk, and the service it had been to her, and she thought that the cat on the milk-jug would remind Popsey of the little black kitten of which she had been so fond.

All these parcels were put carefully under the seat in the pony carriage, and then they drove to Mother Manikin's.

Who should open the door but Betsey Ann, looking the picture of happiness, and dressed very neatly in a clean calico dress, and white cap and apron. Betsey Ann's slip-shod shoes and her rags and tatters were things of the past; she looked an entirely different girl.

'La, bless you!' she cried, when she saw Rosalie; 'I'm right glad to see you again.' And then she suddenly turned shy, as she looked at the two young women, and led the way to the parlour where Mother Manikin was sitting.

The old woman was full of the praises of her new

maid, and Betsey Ann smiled from ear to ear with delight.

'Are you happy, Betsey Ann?' whispered Rosalie, as May was talking to Mother Manikin.

'Happy!' exclaimed Betsey Ann, 'I should just think I am! I never saw such a good little thing as she is. Why, I've been here a whole week, and never had a cross word, I declare I haven't; did you ever hear the like of that?'

'Oh, I am so glad you are happy!' said Rosalie.

'Yes, He—I mean the Good Shepherd—*has* been good to me,' said Betsey Ann. 'But wait a minute, Rosalie,' she said, as she saw that Rosalie was preparing to go; 'I've got a letter for you.'

'A letter for me!' exclaimed Rosalie; 'who can it be from?'

'I don't know,' said Betsey Ann; 'it came the day after you left, and I kept it, in the hope of being able to send it some day or other. I just happened to be cleaning the doorstep when the postman brought it. Says he, "Does Miss Rosalie Joyce live here?" So I says, "All right, sir, give it to me"; and I caught it up quite quick, and I poked it in my pocket. I wasn't going to let her get it. I'll get it for you if you'll wait a minute.'

When Betsey Ann came downstairs she put the letter in Rosalie's hand. It was very bad and irregular writing, and Rosalie could not in the least imagine from whom it had come.

The letter began thus:

'MY DEAR MISS,

'I hope this finds you well, as it leaves me at present; but not so poor Toby who once you knew. Leastways,

I hope he is well, because he is in a better place than this; but he has been very badly off a long while, and last Saturday he died.

'But he told me where you lived; he said you was his master's daughter, and it was you as taught him about the Good Shepherd. I told him, as I was one of his mates, I would write, and tell you he died quite happy, knowing that his sins was forgiven.

'He was a good lad, was Toby. We was a very bad lot when he came to our concern; but he read to us, spelling out the words quite slow like, every evening; and there's a many of us that is like new men since we heard him.

'There was one piece he read quite beautiful, and never so much as spelt a word. It was about the Shepherd looking for a sheep, and bringing it home on His shoulder.

'And he would talk to us about that as good as a book, and tell of a picture he had seen in your caravan, and what you used to teach him about it.

'And just before he died, says he, "Tom, write and tell Miss Rosie; she'll be glad like to hear I didn't forget it all." So now I've wrote, and pardon my mistakes, and the liberty.

'From yours truly,
'THOMAS CARTER.'

Rosalie was very thankful to receive this letter; she had often wondered what had become of poor Toby; and it was a great comfort to her to know that he had not forgotten the lessons they had learned together in the caravan. It was very pleasant to be able to think of him, not in a theatre or a lodging-house, but in the home above, where her own dear mother was.

. . . . .

Rosalie did not grow tired of her green pasture, nor did she wish to wander into the wide world beyond. As she grew older, and saw from what she had been saved, she became more and more thankful.

She was not easily deceived by the world's glitter and glare and vain show; for Rosalie had been behind the scenes, and knew how empty and hollow and miserable everything worldly was.

She had learned lessons behind the scenes that she would not easily forget. She had learned that we must not trust to outward appearances. She had learned that aching hearts are often hidden behind the world's smiling faces. She had learned that there is no real, no true, no lasting joy in anything of this world. She had learned that whosoever drinketh of such water—the water of this world's pleasures and amusements—shall thirst again; but she had also learned that whosoever drinketh of the water which the Lord Jesus Christ gives, even His Holy Spirit, shall never thirst, but shall be perfectly happy and satisfied. She had learned that the only way of safety, the only way of true happiness, was to be found in keeping near to the Good Shepherd, in hearkening to His voice, and in following His footsteps very closely.

All these lessons Rosalie learnt by her PEEP BEHIND THE SCENES.